"Darlin', you know who you want. you've made that real clear all night. You just don't know *what* you want." He leaned a forearm on the bar and then casually traced the whitestrap that showed at the edge of her sweater. "Consider this a warning, Emily, you got my attention. I don't have to like you to want you. And if you keep playing this game, I'm going to do something about it."

"I'm playing the part you assigned me," she reminded him in a whisper. She couldn't pull back because he still had a finger in the neckline of her sweater.

"You're playing at being a bad girl. But that's okay. I like bad girls. They take what they want because it makes 'em feel alive."

He straightened up, satisfied with the effect of his words. Her breathing had quickened and her green eyes were wide. "I'll tell you one more thing. I also like good girls who play at being bad. Cause when they're bad, it's just for me."

WHAT ARE *LOVESWEPT* ROMANCES?

They are stories of true romance and touching emotion. We believe those two very important ingredients are constants in our highly sensual and very believable stories in the LOVE-SWEPT line. Our goal is to give you, the reader, stories of consistently high quality that may sometimes make you laugh, sometimes make you cry, but are always fresh and creative and contain many delightful surprises within their pages.

Most romance fans read an enormous number of books. Those they truly love, they keep. Others may be traded with friends and soon forgotten. We hope that each LOVESWEPT romance will be a treasure—a "keeper." We will always try to publish

LOVE STORIES YOU'LL NEVER FORGET
BY AUTHORS YOU'LL ALWAYS REMEMBER

The Editors

Loveswept ®757

HOT AS SIN

DEBRA DIXON

BANTAM BOOKS
NEW YORK · TORONTO · LONDON · SYDNEY · AUCKLAND

HOT AS SIN

A Bantam Book / September 1995

ISBN 0-553-44499-9

Published simultaneously in the United States and Canada

Bantam Books are published by Bantam Books, a division of Bantam Doubleday Dell Publishing Group, Inc. Its trademark, consisting of the words "Bantam Books" and the portrayal of a rooster, is Registered in U.S. Patent and Trademark Office and in other countries. Marca Registrada. Bantam Books, 1540 Broadway, New York, New York 10036.

PRINTED IN THE UNITED STATES OF AMERICA

OPM   0 9 8 7 6 5 4 3 2 1

This one is for the
"Steppin' Out Dancers,"
wonderful supportive ladies who remind
me that no one is ever truly tapped out.

Special thanks to:

Jack Berry,
my favorite law enforcement official.

Carin Rafferty, Patricia Keelyn,
Martha Shields, Carolyn McSparren,
Lisa Turner, Carol Anne Stone,
and Pam Ireland.
Thanks for everything.

Judy Pierce, thanks for the cat.

PROLOGUE

Deputy Marshal Patrick Talbot keyed the radio again. "Dano, give me a sitrep."

When no one answered, Patrick didn't bother to try a third time. He put the radio on the table, pulled the automatic pistol out of his holster, and cocked it. The bullet shifted into place with an efficient, businesslike double click. "Get the lights."

Emily Quinn scrambled to do as he asked. Patrick moved the window shade a tiny bit with the barrel of his gun. After a minute of studying the front, he checked the rear of the farmhouse and the security system keypad. Then he focused on her.

"I want you upstairs, Emily. In the front bedroom. Take my keys just in case, and don't come down until I get you."

She realized what he intended. The front bedroom was the only one above the porch roof. Patrick was giving her an escape route.

"Hey, cheer up. It's probably just a radio on the

fritz," he said as he picked up the phone. "Goddammit! The phone's dead. Upstairs, now! Move!"

Emily moved. Once upstairs and alone in the dark, she sank to the floor beside the bed. The glow-in-the-dark hands of the Lucite clock ticked off seconds like hell's metronome.

Ten minutes of purgatory passed before she heard the shots. Three of them, close together. And then nothing. Only the sound of the farmhouse breathing and shifting. The sound of an empty house and old trees in the wind. Indecision and fear paralyzed her.

Instinct told her to get out the window, to follow Patrick's unspoken advice and run. But the eerie silence flayed her conscience. What if Patrick were bleeding and too weak to call out? What if he needed help? She couldn't just leave him to die.

Carefully she opened the door and peered into the hallway. Her heart pounded so hard she could feel the surge of blood in her fingertips as she eased her way toward the stairs. When she reached the landing she froze. Below her one man leaned over another, his gun hanging loosely from his hand. In the dark and from her angle she wasn't sure which man was Patrick. Then she registered the brown hair, the suit, the silver-plated gun.

"Patrick," Emily whispered as she walked down the stairs. Relief flowed through her like a sedative. "Thank God, you're alive."

At her voice the man cocked his head and straightened. When he turned around slowly and leveled his gun at her, Emily realized her mistake. But it was too late.

When the gun went off, she didn't even scream. She

closed her eyes. Not because she was brave; because she was a coward. But the bullet never ripped through her. Instead, the gunman made a sound as if someone beat the air out of his lungs with a baseball bat.

Forcing her eyes open, she watched the man pitch forward and stumble into the bottom stair. Patrick's bullet must have hit him square in the back. By the time he tried to catch himself, it was too late. With a sickening thud his head connected with the hardwood spindle of the railing. He didn't move again.

"Emily." Patrick lay at the bottom of the stairs.

Please, God, don't let Patrick die, Emily prayed. She inched past the gunman, afraid to look at him, afraid he'd open his eyes and grab her.

A sweet, cloying smell assaulted her as she shoved aside the overturned card table and knelt at Patrick's side. The front of his shirt was wet with blood. He lay on the cards which had been scattered like confetti. Drinks and chips littered the floor as well. Emily swallowed hard and fought the nausea. She tried not to think of Patrick's life seeping into the carpet just as surely as the spilled soda had.

"What do I do? Just tell me. I'll do it."

He rolled his head a little and made a negative sound. The gun slid out of his hand and onto the floor.

"I've got to stop the bleeding," she said more to herself than to him. She scanned the room for something to use as a pressure bandage.

"Too late." Patrick coughed.

"No, it's not too late," she insisted, fighting tears.

"Take my wallet . . . inside coat pocket. Now," he ordered. When she had it he said, "You run. You cover your tracks. Don't . . . trust anyone. The man who tried to kill you is a U. S. marshal, and . . . I don't know who else is involved." He paused to catch his breath and closed his eyes for a second. "The dog tag on my key chain . . . take it to Christian Gabriel. He owes me. Tell him I said to make you disappear."

"I'm not going anywhere except for help." She stretched to reach the afghan on the back of the couch to keep him warm.

"There is no help." His tone was final. "Can't trust—"

"You are *not* going to die on me, Patrick," Emily interrupted, fighting to keep the fear out of her voice. "I won't let you. You hear?"

"Shut up and listen," he hissed. "Last Call—a bar . . . Rock Falls. In Washington State." He struggled. "Find Gabe. Christian . . . Gabriel. Ex-SEAL, retired, owes me. You got it?"

"I've got it." She took a deep shuddering breath to steady herself. He was close to dying. "Washington. Rock Falls. Last Call. Christian Gabriel."

"Best shot. Targets, pool, people—" He coughed again, the sound ominous. *"Emily?"*

"I'm here. I'm listening." She held both of his hands, trying to rub the cold out of them, trying to rub life back into his body somehow. "I'm here."

"Don't tell . . . the Archangel I caught a bullet. Thinks I'm . . . invincible."

"I won't say a word," she promised.

"Emily."

"Yes?"

"Shoot him." His breathing was raspy, as if he were sucking in air but not getting any oxygen.

Slowly Emily realized what Patrick meant. Her gaze flew to the gunman. The man wore a bulletproof vest; he was only stunned by the fall. If she didn't kill him, he'd come after her and try again.

"Shoot . . . him."

Emily picked up the gun.

ONE

The last time Christian Gabriel saw a nun walk into a bar, Sister Mary Joseph McGregor had come to drag him back to the orphanage. The twenty-year-old memory was still so sharp, it brought a twinge of pain to the lobe of his right ear. Gabe rubbed absently at the spot and wondered if the petite nun who hovered at the door of his bar was strong enough to drag anyone anywhere. But he never doubted for a moment that she'd come to drag someone back to the path of righteousness. Why else would she be scrutinizing his customers?

Casting an experienced eye over his crowd, he tried to pick out the poor sinner and couldn't. There wasn't an underage kid or fallen woman in the bunch. In fact, they were all Saturday-night regulars, mostly men who made a living either cutting trees or hauling logs. Gabe frowned, returning his attention to the nun, who wore a modern gray habit and a short veil, which completely covered her hair. A dark gray wool coat was draped over one arm, and she clutched it to her stomach with the other.

Her body language dropped plenty of clues about her uncertainty. Glasses too big for her face obscured her eyes, which alternately scanned the crowd and counted the floor planks. The sight of an apprehensive nun set Gabe on edge. Nuns were usually so firm of purpose. At least the ones he'd known were, the ones who'd run the orphanage and his life until he was eighteen years old.

If she'd been the least bit like *those* nuns, she'd have already snared her sinner and been halfway to Seattle. Sister Mary Joseph never hovered politely around the fringes. Oh, no, she waded right in and got her business done, throwing her considerable girth around in the process. But this nun didn't have any girth to throw around, even if she'd wanted to. She was pale and fragile. No, not fragile. She looked tired, worn thin.

Years of Catholic school instilled a certain amount of unquestioning respect for women who took vows. But she was beginning to make his customers nervous. Nervous customers didn't order drinks.

He needed to send the good sister on her way or kiss tonight's profit good-bye. Profit was one thing he couldn't afford to lose right now. When she looked up again, he willed her gaze in his direction. He planted one hand on his hip and the other on the dark wooden bar; the look he gave her was less than welcoming.

To his surprise, she squared her shoulders like St. George facing a dragon and approached the bar. Gabe heard the collective sigh of relief go through the crowd as she walked past, ignoring them. The noise level slowly increased. Someone punched up an old country song about lying eyes on the jukebox while a masculine voice from the back hollered, "Marsha Jean! I need a beer over here!"

His waitress, a slender blonde wearing a T-shirt emblazoned THE BIGGER THEY ARE . . . , slipped off the only barstool that was occupied. Grabbing the long-necked bottle of beer that he handed her, Marsha Jean gave the nun a conspiratorial wink before she sashayed away. "If Harry tipped worth a damn, he would have had one of these five minutes ago."

The nun watched Marsha Jean's departure without saying a word. Gabe began to wonder if she was going to get to the point before he had to ask her to leave. He braced both hands against the bar. "Well, which is it, Sister? Business or pleasure?"

The moment she turned to face him, he forgot all about asking her anything because she shocked the hell out of him. Nuns were supposed to be older and plain, but she wasn't. Not by a long shot. Even glasses couldn't diminish the impact of clear green eyes fringed with impossibly long lashes. Didn't she know you weren't supposed to look a man in the eye like that unless you meant business?

Her mouth created a whole new category of sin, her bottom lip lush and full. For an instant her tongue peeked out at the corner, and the idea of testing those lips became all too appealing. What a waste, he thought as he dragged himself reluctantly back to reality. His conscience pinched him for the irreverence, but that didn't stop him from embellishing the thought. What an *incredible* waste.

His next realization was that nuns weren't supposed to look so warily at the human race. In particular, he didn't like this one looking at him so distrustfully. She adjusted her glasses as if stalling for time, and then she swept a look down and back up as much of him as she could see above the bar. Gabe got the distinct impression that she disapproved of him; of haircuts that weren't above the ears and off the collar; and of his five o'clock shadow that was a couple of days old by now.

Stepping back and suddenly wary himself, Gabe paused a half-second before he prodded her again. "Can I get you something to drink, Sister?"

She climbed on one of the empty stools and arranged her coat in her lap. "I'll have some juice."

He reached for a clean glass from the racks above him. "Orange or tomato?"

"Tomato."

"One Virgin Mary—" Gabe froze. He cursed silently at his slip and at how easily one little nun could make him so conscious of good and bad. He thought he'd given up feeling guilty. With a shake of his head he reached for the Bloody Mary mix. "Sorry, Sister."

"For what?" she asked distractedly, then gave him a sharp look. "Oh, I see what you mean. Don't worry. If you walked into my place and heard the Scriptures quoted, you wouldn't expect an apology. Well, neither do I, but if you still feel the need to apologize, I suggest you appeal to a higher authority."

He set the glass in front of her. "Why bother? The last time I did, he wasn't listening."

"God helps those who help themselves."

Gabe smiled. This was an old argument. One he'd

had a hundred times in the orphanage. "Those who help themselves don't need God's help."

"No, they don't. They have faith. They don't need proof."

"Ah . . . that explains it. I was never much good with faith."

"It takes practice."

"Oh, I practiced," he assured her softly. "That's how I know I'm not any good at it."

Suddenly the challenge in her expression was gone, replaced by an almost imperceptible regret. With precise, efficient motions she picked up the salt shaker and sprinkled a large quantity of salt into her tomato juice.

"What time is sunrise tomorrow?" she asked abruptly.

"Excuse me?" he said, dragging his eyes away from the sight of her spiking her drink with a lethal dose of sodium.

"I assume the sun is going to come up in Washington tomorrow."

"It always does."

"See there," she insisted quietly as she put down the shaker. "Everyone believes in something. Even you."

Stunned, Gabe realized he'd just been had by a nun. Before he could figure out how to regain the ground he'd lost or why he cared, Marsha Jean drew his attention by waving her fingers in his peripheral vision. "Darlin', if you can terminate this fascinating conversation about theology long enough to get me some drinks . . . well then, I might just be able to serve a few customers, who might pay us, which means you might make payroll this week."

He tossed a white towel on the bar and began to wipe it down. "Haven't missed a payroll yet, Marsha Jean."

"Yeah, but you've come real close. Maybe this week you won't have to cut any trees to do it." She looked at the nun. "The man's got a thing about his timberland. Of course, around here it's like money in the bank, so most people don't get all weepy about thinning it out now and then. Excepting this one here."

"Marsha Jean, I don't pay you to chat with the customers," Gabe told her bluntly. "Have you got an order, or what?"

"When you ask so nicely, how can I refuse?" she asked as she put a round tray on the counter. "Three Jack Blacks with beer backs and three shots of tequila," she rattled off, and turned to the sister. "Now, what's a nice Catholic girl like you doing in a place like this?"

"I'm waiting for someone."

"Waiting for someone in a bar?" Marsha Jean's tone implied everything that was wrong with the scenario without actually criticizing. "All we got around here is lumberjacks, pretend cowboys, and a bartender with attitude. Surely you aren't lookin' for one of these fellas? Except the bartender, they've all been drinkin'!"

The sister smiled. "God finds nothing wrong with spirits as long as they aren't allowed to weaken the spirit."

"Amen, to that!" Marsha Jean giggled. "But we got some pretty weak spirits in this town."

"Order's up," Gabe interrupted as he finished pouring the last shot. "You keep an eye on them, Marsha Jean. I don't want to have to close early tonight."

At his warning the sister leaned forward, eyebrows raised and concern on her face. She cast a glance around, let her attention linger over the empty barstools and the few couples on the tiny dance floor. "It's a quiet crowd. Why would you close early?"

"It wouldn't be by choice, honey," the waitress explained as she pulled the tray toward her. "Around midnight the customers who chase whiskey with beer usually chase the beer with a fight. Chair-throwin' and fight-startin' is sort of a sport in this neck of the woods."

"Oh, I see," the nun said faintly, but a moment afterward her nod of understanding turned into a confused head-shake. "No, I don't see. Why would you have to close because of a fight? Don't you expect an occasional fight?" She looked at Gabe like a fight promoter assessing his potential as a boxer. "Can't you handle it?"

Marsha Jean laughed as she hoisted the tray. "You gals really don't get out much, do you?"

When she walked away to deliver her drinks, Gabe—knowing all too well that nuns didn't get out to bars much—furnished an explanation. "Around here when they fight, it's usually with a broken bottle in one hand and a knife in the other. After I 'handle it,' I might have to drive down to the hospital in Arlington for an X ray or stitches or both."

"Oh, I see," she said again. But the answer didn't seem to satisfy her. Not by a long shot.

She worried her bottom lip with perfect white teeth and watched Marsha Jean deliver the platter of drinks. Gabe followed her gaze to the group of men who looked entirely too edgy to be mixing whiskey and beer. He wasn't any happier about the situation.

Then her gaze shifted to the door, and she began to watch the clock. He couldn't see if her hands were clasped, but Gabe would have sworn she was doing some heavy-duty praying. Puzzled by her reaction, he tried to fathom why she was suddenly so concerned with the time. Traffic began to heat up, and each time the door opened she stared with hope at the new arrivals, as if matching them against a mental picture. Each time she frowned.

An hour later she'd switched to orange juice and to a stool next to the wall, out of Marsha Jean's traffic pattern. She said it was to rest her back, but Gabe decided it was to escape Marsha Jean Petit's questions. His waitress was a hothouse transplant from the South with a heart of gold but not one ounce of subtlety. People who grew up in small southern towns tended to have a warped view of individual privacy. Her questions made the good sister nervous, which confirmed Gabe's suspicions that the good sister had something to hide.

If he'd been less involved in trying to figure out the nun, he might have seen the fight brewing. Instead, his first clue was the unmistakable sound of a beer bottle being smacked against a table edge and turned into a weapon. Instinctively his head whipped around, his eyes searching the scene in front of him to locate the culprit, but everyone in the place was standing up, obscuring his view.

By the time he'd rounded the bar, the crowd was backing away. Some were already out the door. With good reason.

"Dammit," Gabe whispered when he saw what sent all the smart patrons scurrying out into the parking lot or heading for home.

Sawyer Johns and Clayton Dover, normally the best of friends, were circling each other. Both of them had a nasty, decidedly unfriendly gleam in their eye and a hard set to their mouths. If someone had asked him for a list of patrons who could cause serious damage in a fight, these two would have been at the top of his list. Hell, these two *were* his list. Big, mean, ugly drunks. Both of them. That's why he always watched them carefully when they started backing whiskey with beer. Until tonight.

Until a nun with secrets distracted him.

An expectant hush fell over the crowd as he shouldered his way through. The morbid anticipation and excitement that gripped the bystanders was almost palpable. Several of them shot him looks of encouragement, urging him into the fray.

Gabe knew better than to let fools or the first rush of adrenaline trick him into situations too quickly. Military service had taught him something the orphanage never could—patience. He waited. And rolled down his shirtsleeves, protecting his arms as best he could with the thick red flannel.

As he casually buttoned his cuffs, he asked, "You boys care to tell me what's goin' on here?"

Sawyer answered him with a voice so rusty from whiskey that it was more of a hoarse whisper. "Just a little disagreement, Gabe. You don't want a piece of it."

"You're right. I don't." He took the large silver and turquoise ring off his finger and slipped it into his jeans pocket along with the silver chain he wore around his wrist. "Don't suppose I could convince you to take your disagreement outside?"

"Right here suits us fine," Clayton said as he made a halfhearted preliminary lunge, testing his reflexes and Sawyer's.

"Look, I'm asking you nice, boys. Do me a favor and take this to the parking lot before someone ends up bleeding all over my floor."

Neither of the men answered this time. They were too busy circling, measuring the distance, and kicking furniture out of the way to give themselves plenty of room. Their heavy leather work boots crunched the glass on the floor and ground it in.

They outweighed him, but he was taller with more reach. They had knives and broken beer bottles, but he was sober and trained in hand-to-hand-combat tactics. He liked his odds, but he swore that he was going to get around to buying a baseball bat to keep behind the bar. Yeah, that's what he needed. Or a shotgun. Or classier clientele.

"I guess we're going to do this the hard way." Gabe sighed. The bar was about to close early.

He waded in, knowing he needed to take one of them out quickly, and Clayton was closer. In a motion that was second nature, he avoided the drunk's sloppy lunge and slammed his boot heel into the man's knee-cap. The nasty snapping sound reassured Gabe that Clayton wasn't going anywhere but down. The drunk bellowed and folded like a broken lawn chair as Gabe spun to take on the other one.

Sawyer paused at the sight of Clayton crashing to the floor in agony. The crowd was equally impressed.

"Damn, that had to hurt!"

"This ain't a fair fight."

Gabe had to agree. Bar fights never were; integrity seemed to go out the window right alongside sobriety.

"Aw, Clayton, you fool, stay down," exhorted someone in the crowd.

Disbelief made Gabe flick a glance over his shoulder to see if Clayton had actually dragged himself up. The brief moment gave Sawyer the courage to charge, but the crowd ruined his advantage by sucking in a collective gasp. Their warning saved Gabe from a nasty cut as he whipped back around and realized Sawyer was smarter than the average drunk. He led with his knife instead of his chin.

Simultaneously evading the slicing motion and grabbing Sawyer's forearm, Gabe pulled him closer, off balance. Then he twisted Sawyer's arm and bent the wrist back until the pain penetrated his alcohol-fogged senses. Sawyer suddenly grunted in pain and let the knife fall to the floor, but not before Clayton delivered a sledgehammer punch to Gabe's ribcage.

Ignoring the sensation that exploded at his side, Gabe smashed an elbow into Sawyer's cheekbone and sent him reeling. Tired of the game, he rounded on Clayton and added a little character to his face by rearranging his nose with two swift jabs. Then he swept Clayton's feet out from under him and dumped him to the floor again.

"Look! Sawyer's just as stupid as Clayton," someone said. "They shouldn't get up."

Dammit! Gabe thought, turning to Sawyer. The crowd was right. These boys shouldn't get up. They were about to make him angry. He wheeled and planted a boot squarely in the center of Sawyer's chest, drilling him with enough force to send him backward six feet and into a chair that flipped as soon as his butt landed in it.

The crowd loved that, giving him a chorus of "All right, man!" and discussing the fight as though they were watching cable. "Where'd a bartender learn all that stuff anyway?"

"Ben Lawson says he did some time in Leavenworth," someone volunteered loudly as they made space for Clayton, who was crawling toward the door.

"Hell, he ain't never done time in prison! He spent some time in *Lebanon*, for crying out loud! He was one of those Navy SEAL guys they send on rescue missions. That's where he learned all that ninja crap."

By slow degrees Gabe relaxed. When Sawyer stayed down this time, he stepped back and jerked his head toward the door. "I don't want to have to explain the house rules to you again. You take your fights outside, or next time somebody's going to get hurt."

At his intentional understatement, several of the spectators couldn't hold back snorts of appreciation or nervous chuckles. Sawyer glared at a few of them before he staggered to his feet. When he looked at his knife on the floor, Gabe advised softly, "I'd buy a new one if I were you."

Sawyer decided to take his advice.

"The rest of you go on home. The show's over, and

the bar's closed," Gabe said wearily without looking at what was left of the crowd.

Spearing his fingers through his hair to drag it back out of his face, Gabe expelled the tension inside him and a curse in one breath. The adrenaline faded, and a bruised rib made its presence known. Carefully he put a supporting hand over the spot where his ribcage screamed the loudest. He was getting too old to be the only one on his side in a bar fight. His body had thirty-five hard years on it.

He shook his head at Marsha Jean's offer to stay and waved her out with the rest of the stragglers. "Go home and watch your kids sleep."

Tired and hurting, he was in no mood to deal with anything else. So when he found the nun still lingering behind the others and staring at him with the same disappointment he'd seen a hundred times before, he said a few things he shouldn't. "It was a bar fight. Plain and simple. I didn't break the Fifth Commandment. I just bent it a little, so don't start the sermon, Sister. Not all of us are saints."

"I'm not looking for a saint," she assured him. "I'm looking for you."

TWO

Emily Quinn had been too far back in the crowded bar to hear every word said during the fight, but she'd heard enough to get the general drift of the discussion. Her knees had actually buckled for a moment when she realized that the *bartender* had been a Navy SEAL, that—against all logic—he had to be Patrick's *retired* buddy. The photo in Patrick's wallet had been stuck to the plastic and grainy, but it clearly showed a man who was gaunt and tired and emotionless. A spit-and-polish military man. A man she thought would be older by now.

She had elbowed her way through the crowd without any thought to how her behavior might look or where her elbows landed. By the time she had a clear view of the action, one drunk was crawling toward the exit, and the other was in the process of crumpling to the floor. Christian Gabriel was supposed to be retired, but the man had barely broken a sweat.

Suddenly the casual L. L. Bean clothing that had fooled her originally couldn't disguise the military discipline that shaped his reflexes. His opponents had been in no condition to offer resistance, but his feet had still been braced apart, his knees bent, his hands ready. She doubted he'd even realized that people were crowded around watching with varying degrees of awe.

Staring at him, she had remembered something her dad said while she was growing up. *It's not over until I say it's over.* This man was like her father. He didn't walk away until he was ready or sure.

Christian Gabriel might look detached and emotionless, but he wasn't. He was controlled. He kept his emotions on a very tight leash, but he had them. She'd already seen them. Emily wasn't looking for a saint, but she wasn't looking for a man like this either. Unfortunately, she no longer had a choice.

Emily saw surprise flicker in Gabriel's eyes a second before she heard him laugh. The laugh was obviously a mistake. He winced.

"Looking for me? Now, what would a nun want with me?" he asked, his eyes narrowing and studying her.

Suppressing a shiver, Emily realized that he radiated a power that felt every bit as dangerous to her as a loaded weapon. She had an uneasy premonition she'd be damned if she trusted him and dead if she didn't. Her life felt like Russian roulette, and asking for help might be pulling the trigger.

"I'd like an answer, Sister. What's a nun want with me?"

"I'm not—" *A real nun*, she almost blurted out before instinct clamped her mouth shut. Pretending to be a nun had kept her alive and gotten her this far.

Emily pushed up the ill-fitting glasses and smoothed the wrinkles from the shapeless habit as best she could. Irrationally she wanted to be less desperate, more in control. She wanted to look like anything except what she was—on the run.

Taking a deep breath, she said, "I need your help, Mr. Gabriel."

"If you'd come for help, you could've said something when you walked in." Retrieving her coat and purse from the barstool, he held them out to her. "And if it's a donation you want, you're out of luck. I really am broke."

Emily stood her ground, meeting his hard gaze without flinching. She slipped a hand into the pocket of her habit and touched the dog tag. The tag was her proof, but caution kept her from showing it yet or telling him that Patrick was dead. Promises to dead men were easy to ignore.

And there was always the chance he'd want revenge. Revenge wouldn't bring Patrick back or keep her safe. So she told only the beginning of the truth.

"Patrick Talbot sent me."

Every hair on the back of Gabe's neck stood up at the name from his past. He let the coat and purse slide out of his hand and back onto the stool. "What are you talking about?"

"Patrick sent me," she assured him, her voice stronger. "He just didn't tell me Christian Gabriel was the bartender. And you don't look like your picture."

As he listened, Gabe felt the urge to swear. His old SEAL buddy was one of the few people who knew his full name or his retirement address. He owed Patrick.

Patrick sent a nun? Yeah, well . . . she didn't *feel* like a nun, and Gabe was an expert on nuns. More than anything else, she felt like one of Patrick's infamous practical jokes.

"The name's Gabe." He closed the distance between them, towering over her once more. "Exactly what kind of help do you need, Sister?"

"I need to disappear."

Calmly Gabe waited for a laugh and a "gotcha" that never came. He waited for her to pull off the veil and grin. She didn't. The woman in front of him seemed small and frightened, not bursting with a need to spring the punch line.

Gabe frowned, his suspicions working overtime. He studied her for a moment, taking note of the shadows beneath her eyes and the way she leaned against the chair as if she was going to fall down any minute. Not that she would—he also noted the way her chin rose a notch.

Softly he said, "*Patrick* is the U.S. marshal—not me. Making people disappear is his job."

"He can't help me."

"Why not?"

"Trust me. Patrick can't help me," Emily repeated dully.

"How can you be so sure?"

Because he already died trying to protect me.

Before she found a better answer, one of the small windows across the front of the bar exploded inward. Shattered glass flew in all directions. Emily froze in horror, but Gabe reacted.

He grabbed her and dove for the floor, rolling until

they were away from the flying glass. His body formed a shield for hers. Emily fought to slow the beating of her heart which thumped hard in her chest as adrenaline-charged blood pounded through her body and roared in her ears. She didn't realize she was clutching Gabe's shoulders until he rose up slowly, head turned toward the door as if he might go and investigate.

"Don't," she heard herself whisper in a broken voice she hardly recognized as her own. Emily was scared she'd been found, scared someone else was going to be killed protecting her, scared she'd spend the rest of her life feeling this way. "Don't go out there."

Surprisingly gentle Gabe pulled away and drew her up on her knees. He picked up her glasses, which had flown off, and pressed them into her hand. "I'm not going anywhere, but I want you to get behind the bar and stay there. Before anything else happens. And stay down."

She nodded and did what he said, scooting behind the bar and folding herself into a very small ball in the corner—between the big aluminum beer cooler and the wall.

"Please, God, not again. Please, God, not again." Over and over she repeated the short prayer. Bits and pieces of what happened that night in Idaho flashed into her mind.

She was crying when Gabe knelt down beside her. She couldn't stop, even when he raised her chin and wiped the tears that trickled off her jaw.

"Hey, it's all right. It was just a rock. Probably Sawyer's clever idea of revenge for the fight tonight." He helped her up and around the cooler until they were standing by the register. "See? Everything's fine."

"No, it's not," she said raggedly, and stole some comfort by burying her face against his chest. She wasn't strong enough to pretend anymore, and he was warm and real and solid.

Startled by her reaction, Gabe was unprepared for the rush of sensations that swamped him. The pain in his ribs and the woman pressed against him were reminders of why he left the navy to begin with. He was tired of hurting and tired of fighting someone else's battles. He'd done his bit for God and country. He'd spent seventeen years pulling people out of bad situations.

But old habits died hard, and right now—like it or not—she was a woman who needed saving. Slowly his arms went around her, and he rested his chin against the top of her head.

"Shh . . ." The sound wasn't much in the way of a brilliant reassurance, but it was the best he could do.

While he held her, he came to three very important conclusions. First, these tears were the real McCoy and not a melodramatic reaction to tonight's rock-throwing contest. Second, the lady had been terrified when the window shattered, but not surprised. It was almost as though she had expected violence. Third, it appeared that nuns, if she was a nun, didn't have to cut their hair anymore.

Her veil had been knocked askew, revealing a rich brown mane with hints of gold. Free of its pins, her hair spilled down her back in waves. Gabe plucked the veil off and tossed it toward the counter. Then he bracketed her head with his hands and lifted her face to his.

"If you're going to cry all over me, then at least tell me your name." She hesitated a second too long, and Gabe knew she was lying.

"Emma."

"Sister . . . Emma"—he upended the stools that had gone crashing to the floor—"sit."

Then he fixed himself a drink to dull the pain of his ribs. Knowing one wouldn't be enough, he poured a second and set it down. While he was getting orange juice for the sister, she reached for the shot glass. Her hand trembled, but she knocked it back without a gasp or a cough.

My kind of nun, he thought. *One who takes her whiskey neat.*

He set the juice in front of her and left her while he taped a flattened box over the gaping hole in the window.

When he finished, she said, "I—I think I need to splash some water on my face."

He gestured with his head. "Ladies' room is that way."

He strode back toward the bar, waiting only long enough to hear the click of the bathroom door before opening Emma's purse. Ordinarily he'd be the first one to say: If she dresses like a nun, walks like a nun, and talks like a nun, then she must be a nun.

Emma did all of those things. She also downed whiskey like water, obviously lied about her name, didn't need those glasses, and an evening in a smoke-filled bar hadn't bothered her eyes.

A quick tour of her wallet revealed nothing. As he'd half expected, the normal identification—driver's license, social security card, credit cards—were all missing. A photograph of an older couple standing in front of a frozen winter pond was stuck in the currency section, but there were no bills. She had forty-eight cents in the coin pocket.

Setting the wallet down on the counter, Gabe went fishing again. This time with better results. He found six tickets for departures from Boise, Idaho, under six different names. None had been used, and each was dated three days before. Emma was playing a game of fox and hounds with someone.

When he pulled out a small gold case containing a tube of lipstick, Gabe shot a speculative glance at the bathroom door. Her halo was slipping. It finally fell all the way off when he found a receipt from a store called the Necklace Connection. The crucifix around her neck had cost nineteen ninety-five.

"Well, there you have it, folks," he said under his breath. "Innocent Emma is not a nun, and she is definitely on the run. But from what? And why the nun bit?"

As he heard the faucet being turned off, he shoved the contents back in her purse. When she came out of the bathroom, she pulled something out of the side pocket of her skirt and walked toward him, holding it in front of her like an offering.

"Patrick said to give you this as proof."

Gabe reached, but even before he touched it, he realized what it was—the dog tag. *Patrick's dog tag.* The one neatly drilled by a bullet that had been meant for Gabe. The one Patrick kept on his key chain as a reminder that he was invincible, and as a reminder that the Archangel owed him. *Archangel*—a nickname from a lifetime ago and a world away.

Gabe's gaze captured hers, uneasiness stealing over him and leaving a coldness in its wake. "Patrick wouldn't have given you this."

"If there had been any other way, I'm sure he wouldn't have." She didn't let go of the dog tag even though his fingers had closed around it. "He had to move a witness. He couldn't talk about the assignment, and he couldn't stick around to help me. So, is it true?"

"Is what true?" he asked, stalling for time, his mind racing. If Patrick was transporting a hot witness, he could be gone for two days. If he was on the security detail, he could be gone for two weeks. *Or longer.*

"Is this dog tag a promissory note like he said it was?" she asked. The flat metal ID was still suspended between them like a bone between two dogs. "Do you owe him? Anytime, anywhere?"

Frustration rolled through Gabe. He hated the way she'd boxed him into a corner, and he hated the debt he owed Patrick. Physically, the cold metal dog tag weighed almost nothing and yet weighed so heavily on his conscience. For Gabe the bottom line was the same now as it had been ten years ago. How much was his life worth?

"I owe him." The words were tight, forced out of him.

She let go and closed her eyes for a second in relief. "Then keep your promise and don't ask any questions. Make me disappear. Help me create a new identity"— her voice hardened—"and then forget you ever saw me."

"Create a new identity?" Gabe snapped his fingers. "Just like that."

"Patrick said it wouldn't be hard."

"Of course not!" Gabe exploded in disgust. "Patrick was a plank owner—an original member—of SEAL Team Six! He doesn't admit that anything is hard except his head and his—"

His sentence hung in the air, incomplete but mentally finished by both of them in the awkward silence. Emma blushed. Gabe ran his fingers through his hair, pulling it back from his face and tugging slightly in frustration before letting go.

"You want me to break—" he floundered for a number and finally said, "I don't know how many laws for you and then simply forget you?"

"You'll be safer that way."

"Oh, really? According to whom?"

"Patrick. He said to take his advice for once."

One of Gabe's eyebrows shot up involuntarily. *Safer?* Since when had Patrick cared about "safe" in relation to a SEAL? According to him, safe was for paper pushers and ship drivers, not for the men in the teams. Playing it safe ate up time and got you there a half-second too late to do more than present a nice target for the enemy. Patrick didn't care about safe, and he never gave advice. Which meant Patrick was trying to tell him something without the woman knowing.

All Gabe's senses went on alert, but he said nothing to Emma. Instead, he smiled and slipped the dog tag into his shirt pocket. "That's my boy Patrick. Always looking out for me. And for you, it seems. Refresh my memory—which order are you with, *Sister?*"

"I didn't say."

"God help us all." He could hear the deliberate sarcasm in his tone as he goaded her. "Surely that's not classified too?"

She stared back at him without answering.

"Look, it's late," he finally said. "Too late to make you disappear, and definitely too late to send you to a motel in Marysville. Which means you stay here tonight. Upstairs in my apartment. Any objections?"

"No. Does that mean you'll do it? No questions?"

"You have the dog tag. I don't see that I have any choice." *At least not until I hear from Patrick.* "Have you got any bags in the car?"

"No bags. No car either," she explained. "I took the Community Transit bus from Everett."

He marked her purse and her coat with his gaze. The worn wool garment looked like something she'd picked up at a second-rate thrift store. "It's thirty degrees out, and that's all you've got?"

"I'm traveling light."

No, Gabe corrected her silently, *you're running fast.* "Get your stuff and come on."

Emily almost forgot her veil until Gabe pointed it out as he turned off the lights behind the bar. Inwardly cursing herself for the slip, she picked it up. When her eyes adjusted to the darkness, she followed him to a cheap veneer door in the back of the bar by the pay phone. A generic sign that was available at any hardware store read EMPLOYEES ONLY. Gabe unlocked the door and flipped a light switch to the right of the jamb. A narrow wooden staircase doubled back on itself halfway up to the second floor.

When he expected her to go up the stairs ahead of him, Emily balked. The space seemed too small, too much like a trap. Suddenly it didn't matter that Patrick had sent her or that he had vouched for Gabe. Because Patrick was dead, and she was alone with a man she didn't know, staring into a future she couldn't begin to imagine.

For the past three days she'd been able to put one foot in front of the other because she had a goal, an address to reach, a favor to ask. But she hadn't thought beyond that. Resentment mingled with her fear as she realized how much was gone—her parents, a chance for Olympic gold, her skating career, Patrick's life, and now her own.

You didn't care about your career or the gold medal, her conscience whispered. *The ankle was a convenient excuse so you could give up a dream that didn't belong to you.* Right now Emily would have gladly traded the knot of terror in her stomach for another chance at the secondhand dream she'd thrown away.

"Is something wrong?" Gabriel asked when the silence between them grew too heavy.

She walked past him and said, "A better question would be 'Is anything right?'"

"I usually am," he said. When she reached the landing, he told her, "Like now. You need more than sleep. How long since you've eaten?"

Emily froze without answering. She was eye to eye with the largest Himalayan cat she'd ever seen. He sat enthroned on the top step like a weary pharaoh surveying his minions as they came to pay homage. Bored china-blue eyes blinked in her direction before moving past her to Gabe. His fluffy tail slowly swished around to drape artfully over the edge of the stair, and then he reproached his owner for tardiness with a second pointed twitch of his tail.

For the first time in what seemed like months, Emily smiled. She shifted her coat and purse so she could let the cat sniff her fingers as she got closer. "Hello there," she crooned.

The cat bumped her fingertips with the tip of his nose. The contact was quick and soft and cool. Then he made a noise that could be described only as dismissal and led the way into the apartment.

A pool table dominated the front half of the large room. It shared the space with a couch and armchair that were more upholstered lumps than furniture. From the dishes piled on the coffee table, she'd found the dining room. A vented wood stove occupied a nearby corner, flanked by two wood bins.

"What's his name?" she asked as the cat circled around to rub his body against Gabe's leg.

"Wart." At her disappointed look, he said, "I inherited him from the previous owner. The man's grandchildren promised Gramps the cat could live out his days here."

"You seem to get along."

"I wanted the bar, and I couldn't have one without the other." The cat jumped up onto the king-size bed across the room. "Gramps called him King Arthur."

Emily caught the connection—Wart, Merlin's name for Arthur in the Camelot legend. More evidence that Gabe didn't fit neatly into the humorless, macho military stereotype she'd expected.

He was younger than Patrick. From the experience lines at the corners of his eyes, she guessed thirtysomething. His body, honed to efficient perfection by the demands of his past, looked at least a decade younger than his face.

Wondering what other skills Gabe had honed to perfection in his past, she shot an involuntary glance at the bed. All at once the most important detail of his apartment registered. On the far side of the room sat Gabe's big bed with its bookcase headboard. One shelf held CDs, and on the top was a stack of what looked like a week's worth of newspapers that hadn't been unfolded, much less read. She didn't see a television, but computers and other electronic gadgets lined one wall along with a file-cluttered desk.

Her eyes swept the apartment one last time, making sure she hadn't made a mistake. The two open doors by the kitchen alcove led to the bathroom and a closet. There was no guest room.

How could she keep up the pretense of being a nun if she was constantly in his sight? Sooner or later she'd make the sign of the cross backward.

"It's one big room," she stammered.

"Don't worry, Sister," Gabe promised as he pried her coat and purse from her grip.

Emily wanted to laugh. Not worry? Not likely. Fooling strangers on the street for a minute or two was easy. All she'd had to do was smile and nod. Fooling Gabe was a different matter altogether, and maybe unnecessary. But she couldn't rid herself of the idea that the less she told anyone, the better her chances. *The better their chances.*

"I know this is close quarters for you," Gabe apologized, "but it's the best I can do for tonight. I'll sleep on the couch and give you as much privacy as I can."

She watched him hang her coat and purse on a rack just inside the entrance. Mentally she measured the distance from bed to couch again. She knew it wouldn't be far enough to hide her nightmares from him. Worst of all, Emily wasn't sure she could sleep with someone else in the room. She felt the most vulnerable when her eyes closed.

Since Idaho, every soft sound was the scrape of a shoe against carpet. Every creak was a floorboard protesting the weight of a silent gunman. She was suddenly six years old again and afraid of a real-live bogeyman. She couldn't sleep with her back to the door or if the closet was open. She couldn't sleep without turning on the bathroom light or until she'd checked the dead bolt at least five times.

"Hey, Sister Emma. Come back." When she snapped out of her reverie, Gabe suggested, "Why don't you take a shower while I heat some soup?"

"Oh, no. This isn't what Patrick meant when he said you'd take care of everything. All I need is—"

"To slow down long enough to think about what you're doing." As he talked he strode to the closet and paused a half-beat to make a selection. He pulled a navy blue polo shirt off a hanger.

"Here. This ought to cover you almost to the knees. Shampoo and soap are on the edge of the tub. The towel's been used once, but it's the closest thing to clean that I've got right now. Next time have Patrick phone ahead. When you come out you can toss your clothes in the washer and your butt in bed, or you can take my advice and eat some soup first."

Emily didn't move, unsure how a nun would react to Gabe's offer. She knew how she felt—overwhelmed. Yes, she'd love the chance to stand in a warm shower until the tension knots in her shoulders disappeared, but not in his shower. Doing that would create some kind of bond. You couldn't wear a man's shirt without letting him inside your defenses a little. By the time she finished that shower and put on his shirt, she'd be enveloped by his scent, the textures of his life.

Instinct that had nothing to do with survival warned that she was much too susceptible to Gabe on a sensual level. His intensity called to her hormones, and that was dangerous. Christian Gabriel was a means to an end and nothing more.

"Don't you have a robe or something?" she asked nervously.

"No, I don't," Gabe answered. "Think of me as your brother, or, better yet, a Jesuit. The only thing they care about is a good argument, being right, and the search for truth and knowledge. Hit the shower, Emma," he ordered, tossing the shirt at her. "No disrespect, but I don't think we need to call any more attention to you than necessary," he added. "So I'll drop the 'Sister' for now, and tomorrow we'll get you new clothes for the same reason."

"But you don't understand. I can't—"

"Tomorrow. Let it go until tomorrow." He herded her toward the bathroom, flipped on the light, and closed the door after he nudged her in.

When his footsteps faded away, Emily locked the

door and leaned heavily against it. Her breath rushed out in an audible sigh of frustration. He wanted her to ditch the habit because he thought it drew too much attention!

He had no idea how wrong he was.

The drab gray outfit had become a uniform of invisibility, a crutch. Without it and the glasses, she might be recognized. Emily's heart stopped as she caught sight of herself in the mirror.

She'd forgotten to put back on the glasses.

Gabe didn't waste time. At most he had ten minutes to figure out how much rope to give Emma. In that same ten-minute time frame he had to produce dinner and send a fax to Patrick. He grabbed cans and pans and managed to get dinner squared away and heating on the stove in record time.

The fax took a bit longer because he was walking a very fine line with no solid information to guide him.

FACT: Patrick had sent her.

FACT: She was scared.

FACT: Emma wasn't a nun.

FACT: If Gabe wanted to, he could help her disappear.

He had the skills, but that's what bothered him most about the situation. If all Patrick wanted was to help her vanish, he certainly didn't need Gabe's help. There were plenty of people he could have called on. So why hadn't he? Why waste the dog tag on something like this? Why plant all those clues?

Simple, Gabe realized. Patrick didn't want Emma to

vanish. He was trusting Gabe to baby-sit until he could shake this assignment and handle it himself.

"So what the hell am I supposed to do with her while I'm waiting for you to show up?" Gabe mumbled. If Emma suspected he was trying to slow her down, she'd try disappearing on her own. "And what the hell is your connection to Emma?"

Conscious of the fleeting time, Gabe made some quick decisions. He dialed into a large oil corporation's computer system and logged on. Computer technology was a hobby of his, another leftover from the military. The SEAL teams, especially Six, which was the counterterrorist unit, had wonderful collections of toys. His private gadgets weren't quite in the same league with Six's, but they'd do.

He wrote out a cryptic message on a piece of paper, using a phrase that he'd said every time he'd fallen victim to one of Patrick's plots. The fax wouldn't mean much to anyone else, but Patrick would figure it out.

Well, Patrick, old buddy, this is another fine mess you've gotten me into. As you might have guessed, the special Christmas present you ordered has finally arrived. Instead of forwarding it to the final destination, I thought I might hold on to it until we can get together and decide how to wrap it. Call me.

He took a few seconds to reprogram his fax machine so the originating phone number would be omitted and sent the message through. As soon as his message showed up on the oil company's computerized fax log, he opened the file, keyed in the fax number for Patrick's office, and rerouted it to the send queue. For all intents and purposes, this document would look like it had been created on a computer in New York.

Shower curtain rings jingled against the metal rod as the curtain was flung back. Gabe was out of time, and so was Emma. He positioned the mouse pointer and clicked the send button.

THREE

Behind him, Gabe heard the whoosh of the bathroom door opening but kept his attention on the soup. His fax was tucked safely away in his files since he was leery of leaving it in the trash. Clanking a spoon against the edge of one of the pans, he said, "The washer's in here. I set the detergent out."

"Thank you." She padded almost noiselessly across the linoleum.

He resisted the temptation to turn around until he heard the rustle of her clothes as she stuffed them into the washer before he sneaked a peak. All he could see was her back. That was more than enough to make him recant every curse he'd heaped on Patrick's head for this mysterious baby-sitting detail.

Emma's shapeless gray dress had been replaced by his shirt. She leaned into the washer, rearranging something, and the bottom edge of the shirt crept up, showing an increasing amount of smooth, creamy, well-exercised thigh. For such a small woman, she had way too much leg, he decided.

As his gaze traveled upward, he felt his mouth go dry. Despite being oversize, the knit shirt molded itself to her body as she stretched, outlining the curve of her hips and rump. Every swell, every valley. *Innocent Emma wasn't wearing a damn thing under that shirt!* His body reacted with an involuntary tightening and a little rush of satisfaction—an intuitive acknowledgment from his hormones that the chase was on whether he wanted it to be or not.

When she finished sprinkling in the powder and closed the lid, Gabe made himself turn back to the stove, as much to hide his body's reaction as to give her privacy. "The permanent-press cycle doesn't work, so you'll have to use the other one."

The dial protested as she cranked it around and pushed it in to start the water. "That's all right. You could beat this habit on a rock, and it wouldn't make any difference. Polyester is made to last."

"Like your vows," Gabe commented, unable to resist. But he spared her having to lie by asking, "What'll you have? Chicken noodle warmed up straight from the can? Or tomato soup, which I confess to doctoring with my own secret ingredients?"

Still facing away from him, she pulled off the towel and let her long, wet hair fall down her back as she shook her head gently. "Chicken noodle, please."

Gabe ladled the soup into a black stoneware bowl and added crackers to the plate beneath her bowl. When she stepped up beside him she held the towel in front of her with one hand, like a limp shield. With the other, she self-consciously raked her fingers through her hair to tame it into some semblance of order while it dried. Everything about her was fresh and new and vulnerable.

For a split second Gabe got lost in the details of the woman. In the bar she had been weary and shapeless with only her eyes and mouth hinting at her sensuality. After her shower she had remembered to put the big glasses back on, but they couldn't hide the color in her cheeks or the smoothness of her skin. The shirt was open at the neck, and he could see the sheen of moisture that still clung to the hollow of her throat.

"You shouldn't have gone to so much trouble," she said in that soft I-don't-want-to-cause-any-problems voice of hers.

Too late for that now, he thought as he found a spoon and slipped it into her bowl.

"I was hungry too." He lifted the plate and handed it to her, caught off guard for a moment. When she smiled at him, it wasn't a sensual pleasure, but a comfortable pleasure, warm and inviting. Surprising himself as much as Emma, he confessed an unfamiliar longing. "For once I won't have to eat alone."

At his words, he thought he saw a tiny spark of empathy flare to life in her eyes, but it was gone as quickly as it had appeared. She swung away from him toward the couch and the newly cleared coffee table. "Company is always nice."

"You're probably used to it." He picked up his own dishes and followed.

"Not really."

"Oh?" Gabe smiled. Tripping her up was going to be like taking pistol practice with a bazooka. As easy as one, two, boom. "I thought nuns did most things in a community . . . as a group."

When her back stiffened, Gabe counted his comment as a direct hit. Funny thing though—he discovered he was rooting for her to make the game interesting. *You be careful, darlin'. Don't dig a deeper hole.*

Before answering, Emma managed a graceful maneuver that ended with her sitting on the couch and the towel draped modestly across her legs like a tablecloth. The plate rested on her knees, and she stirred the soup, blowing a bit to cool it. More like stalling for time, Gabe decided.

She raised her head. "We nourish our souls as well as our bodies during meals. For my order, dinner is a time of silent reflection."

Gabe felt like applauding, but refrained. "Oh, I see. Well then, do you mind if we talk? Will you break a rule if we do?"

"N-no. I'm not at the convent. We could skip a custom or two, with no harm done."

"Surely you're not going to skip the blessing?" he asked, biting the inside of his jaw to keep from laughing at the evil look she shot him before she managed to recover.

"Of course not." Emma muddled through a vague sign of the cross and clasped her hands for a quick prayer, obviously determined to brazen out her charade.

At the end of her generic blessing Gabe intoned, "Amen."

"Amen," she echoed softly, and dug into her soup with a vengeance.

Good strategy, he decided, since she couldn't say

anything wrong with a mouth full of food. He took a few bites of his own while he studied her, puzzled at her haste. If soup was a strategy, then she should be eating slowly, dragging out the chewing and swallowing process. But she wasn't; she was hungry.

Angry with Patrick for not looking after her better, he asked, "How long since you've eaten? Exactly?"

Her spoon stopped mid-trip, dripping translucent yellow broth back into the bowl. The spoon inched toward her mouth, as if she considered finishing the bite first. Then she sighed and set it back in the bowl.

When her chin came up, Gabe chided gently, "Careful, Emma. Fibbing is a waste of time, not to mention a sin."

Emily wet her lips and then wished she hadn't broadcast her nervousness. The way he looked at her made her feel as if she were wearing her soul on the outside. She wondered how many young sailors had spilled their guts when confronted with that relentless gaze and a large chunk of oppressive silence.

"Three days," she finally admitted.

"Three days!"

"I was fasting," Emily improvised.

Gabe set his bowl on the coffee table and leaned forward. His gaze sharpened, warning her to be careful. She got the distinct impression he was closing in for the kill. "How much money do you have?"

"Enough," she lied. "Not that more money wouldn't give me peace of mind. If you want to help, I'd be happy to work in exchange—"

"Sorry, Emma. You heard Marsha Jean. I'm all

tapped out at the moment. I can barely pay the employees I have."

"I see," Emily said. His answer meant she'd have to pawn the lipstick case. It was solid gold, a gift from her grandfather. Dredging up a peaceful nunlike smile, she said, "God will provide."

"If you're waiting for God to provide, *Sister*, then He better start providing pronto." He settled back in his chair and drilled her with a satisfied look. "Forty-eight cents isn't enough to buy an instant cup of coffee, much less an instant new life."

Violation was the first emotion to surface, sharp and hot and intense. "You went through my *purse* when I was in the shower?"

"Of course not. I went through your purse when you were in the bathroom downstairs. Emma, think for a minute. You're in my house. I'd be a fool not to check you out. And Patrick wouldn't have sent you here if I were a fool. Do you trust him?"

"Yes." There was still anger in her voice.

"Then trust me. I owe him my life. I can't think of much I wouldn't do if he asked. That's what this dog tag is about. That's why there's a hole in it. Because he took a bullet that was meant for me."

Gabe laughed hollowly, the sound more a huff than a true laugh. "Sounds so easy when I say it like that, doesn't it? 'Took a bullet.' Well, there is nothing easy about it."

No, there isn't, Emily echoed silently as she closed her eyes and wished she could forget.

"The bullet drilled a hole in his dog tag and nicked his lung." He rubbed a spot on his chest, just to the right of his sternum, as if he could feel the impact, and then dropped his hand. "He almost bled to death before we could get him to the extraction site and on the chopper."

Gabe shifted uncomfortably in the chair. "Patrick never complained though. He thought bleeding to death was a fair trade since the alternative had been to let the bullet ventilate my head. I'll spare you the sad, sorry history of my life, but suffice it to say that Patrick is about the only person who ever thought my life worth saving. Most everyone else, including the navy—especially the navy—thought I was expendable or just plain not worth the effort."

"But your family—"

"Darlin', I grew up in an orphanage. I don't have any family."

Except maybe a dead man, Emily thought, and wished she didn't care that Gabe was alone now that Patrick was dead.

Silence surrounded them, filled the space between them until there was only awkwardness. Gabe couldn't stand the quiet. He picked up his dishes and took them to the kitchen.

When he returned, Emma was staring at her empty bowl, lost in thought. As gently as he could, he reached over and picked up her plate, accidentally pulling the towel with it. She didn't bother to tug the shirt lower or grab the towel for modesty. Instead, she raised her eyes to his. Even through the glasses they were suspiciously shiny, as if they were about to drop tears.

"Ah, hell," he swore softly as he pushed the coffee table out of the way and set her dishes on it. Without taking his gaze from hers, he pulled her to her feet. "You *can* trust me, Emma."

Emily was keenly aware of the sincerity in Gabe's promise. He stood over her, not threateningly close, but close enough that she had to tilt her head back. His dark eyes never wavered from hers, silently urging her to believe him.

Everything decent inside her rebelled against the secret she kept, urging her to tell him the truth. He deserved to know that his only family was dead. Keeping it from him was the worst kind of deceit. But after hearing him talk about Patrick, she was also more certain than ever that the warrior in Gabe would want revenge.

If she told him how Patrick died, he'd move heaven and earth to get justice. He might even use her as bait to get it. That thought hardened her resolve, but his hand was still at her elbow, his thumb rubbing her arm in reassurance.

In a fuzzy second, what was between them changed from an issue of trust to an issue of elemental attraction. The contact of his thumb against her skin as he slipped it beneath the edge of her shirt-sleeve made her aware of the current arcing between them. And of the fact that she wore nothing beneath the knit shirt except skin.

With a simple touch he had opened Pandora's box, and all her pent-up hormones had come rushing out to play. Adrenaline that had nothing to do with fear began to set the pace for her pulse. In an unexplained phenomenon the room closed in around her, pushing her toward him, and the floor seemed to tilt, making her unsteady on her feet. As she braced for the inevitable contact, Emily placed her hand against his chest.

Right until the moment she touched him, Gabe thought he was in control. The quicksilver surge of desire that spiked through him was ample proof that he wasn't. He used every mental control technique he knew to keep his hands to himself and his lips off hers. He wanted to kiss Emma, but he had this unfortunate rule about taking advantage of half-starved women in trouble. He didn't. No matter how much he wanted to.

Sidestepping without letting go of her arm, he ordered huskily, "Come on. That's it for tonight. It's lights-out for you." Almost before she opened her mouth to object, he cut her off roughly. "Don't argue with me, Emma. I'm not in the mood. You're sleeping in the bed, and I'll take the couch. Got it?"

She nodded. His tone hadn't left her much choice as he hustled her across the room.

"Good. Tomorrow we can arm-wrestle for the bed if that will make you happy."

Gabe turned down the bed, held the covers, and waited for her to slip beneath the sheet and blankets. Never looking him in the eye, Emma sank down on the bed, simultaneously taking the covers from him and whisking her legs from view. But not fast enough to keep his attention from getting all tangled up with the tan legs that he'd tried to ignore for the past twenty minutes. Emma's toenails were a pale shimmery pink.

Dragging his mind back from a train of thought that would only complicate his life further, Gabe reached toward her to slip her glasses off so she could lie down.

"No!" Emma's hand flew up to stop him. "I'll do it."

Slowly she took them off herself and put them behind her on the bookshelf. Gabe noticed how she let her hair fall forward and kept her face angled away from him. He'd already seen her without the glasses. So why hide now?

He leaned across her to dislodge the cat and retrieve the second pillow. As he dragged it toward him, he made a mental note to work on the question. Gabe stood up and switched off the lamp on top of the bookcase headboard.

"Good night . . . Emma," he said, and picked up the spare velour blanket from the foot of the bed.

"Good night," Emily whispered as she snuggled down into the covers, turning so that she faced the closet. It was still open, a black gaping hole in the room.

Without raising her head she listened for Gabe's movements. First he fiddled with the wood stove. When the lights went out, she heard the sound of boots hitting the floor, and the whisper of a belt being pulled through trouser loops. The blanket snapped as he unfurled it, and the couch groaned under his weight. He punched the pillow twice.

And when he was finally settled, the real night began. Her two familiar enemies—silence and the darkness—began to smother her. Slowly she counted to ten as she breathed in and out, hoping the routine would stop her heart from racing.

She had to act normal. *Breathe in.* The dark was the worst. *Breathe out. Breathe in. Breathe out.* . . .

When she couldn't stand it anymore, she sat up. "Gabe?"

"Hmm," he said, half asleep.

"Do you mind if we leave the bathroom light on?"

She added a lie because she was afraid her request sounded silly. "In case I have to get up in the middle of the night."

"No," his voice was raspy. "I don't mind."

"Thank you."

Gabe opened his eyes and frowned at the ceiling. Her reply was more like a huge sigh of relief than a polite response. Something was wrong. Rising up quietly on his elbow, Gabe noticed that not only did she turn on the bathroom light, she carefully closed the closet door and began checking the windows by the bed. If she could have gotten to the door downstairs without risking his attention, Gabe was sure she would have checked it too.

When she paused at the second window, he eased himself to a sitting position, clasping his arms around his drawn-up knees. "Something wrong, Emma?"

She jumped with a startled exclamation and whirled toward him. "No. No, everything's fine."

"The windows are locked, Emma. And so are the doors. I checked 'em twice."

"Oh, I wasn't worried about that," she lied. "I was just noticing how dark it is away from the city."

"What city is that?"

"Any city." She dragged her shirt down in the back as if he could not only see in the dark but behind her as well.

"Let's see. No specific city. No specific convent. No specific past. I'll bet you even have generic fingerprints."

Emma didn't rise to the bait. She crawled back into

the bed and scooted under the covers. "I've already explained everything I can, Gabe."

"Funny. I don't recall any explanations." Gabe lay back down and stared at the ceiling. "And so far I haven't seen any sign of trust."

A long time later, so softly he could barely hear her, Emma whispered, "I'm not really a nun."

"I know." Gabe closed his eyes and said, "Now go to sleep."

Instinct woke him.

Gabe opened his eyes to blackness and waited for his senses to talk to him. A second later they did. The rustle of sheets betrayed Emma as she wrestled with the night.

Part of him wanted to pretend he had never heard the troubled sound and go back to sleep. But another part of him was drawn to Emma by the need to reassure her. By the time Gabe shook his legs free of the blanket, Emma's first soft moan reached his ears.

He swore silently at the way he kept jumping right back into all the old habits tonight. Well, he scoffed as he maneuvered quietly around the couch, why the hell should he change now?

Most of his life had been spent rushing in where angels feared to tread. His career as a troublemaker at the orphanage had been long and distinguished. Being a Navy SEAL had simply been a more mature way of saying "Hey, look at me. I'm clever. I deserve your attention."

As he approached the bed, Gabe felt the quickening of his pulse. His instincts told him that Emma and danger were a package deal. Despite all his talk of being retired, Gabe was hooked on the rush he got from teetering on the edge, pushing his ability to control a bad situation. He liked taking the point, being responsible. It was the one troublesome character flaw he'd picked up at the orphanage and that the navy had encouraged.

You're a fool, Gabe told himself, looking down at Emma. She'd gone quiet for a moment. *You were a fool at eighteen and you're a fool now. Always wanting what you can't have.*

At eighteen he'd fooled himself into thinking he could make a place for himself in the navy. He'd fought and clawed his way into officer country, only to find out he didn't have the secret decoder ring, the one given to every graduate of the Naval Academy. Without that class ring he would always be an "untouchable," an expendable junior officer.

Christian Gabriel was very good at killing terrorists, but not flagship material. He was a SEAL, a snake-eater. Therefore, no Pentagon staff assignment. No war college. No stars in his future.

So he took their early-out money and walked away. He swore that the world would have to get along without him. Swore he was through jumping through hoops for crumbs. And then Patrick sent Emma, who needed a hero, even in her sleep.

She was growing restless again. Even in the scant light provided by the bathroom, he could see worry furrowing her brow as she battled invisible demons. He didn't like having to stand idly by while Emma suffered, but waking her up might scare her more.

The hero business was a dangerous one, Gabe decided. The real risk wasn't the bad guys; it was Emma. He was attracted to her, and that attraction couldn't go any further. It would only complicate both their lives when she disappeared or when Patrick came to get her.

"Well, Patrick," Gabe quoted quietly as he thought of his friend, "this is another fine mess you've gotten me into."

At his words, Emma's soft moan escalated into an urgent plea full of dread and disbelief and helplessness. The sound tore at Gabe's gut and froze him in place. Whatever she saw in the shadows of sleep was linked to the sadness and desperation that haunted her eyes. He'd stake his life on it. Unable to watch her distress any longer, he reached out to wake her.

Emma screamed before he touched her.

FOUR

"*No!*"

Emily came awake and bolted upright in bed at the same instant, shuddering and filled with a terror that was too real this time. The dream was always over the minute she screamed, but tonight waking up didn't make the dream vanish. Just as clearly as if she were trapped in sleep, she could see the blood seeping between her fingers.

Putting her head in her hands, Emily tried to stop the images from coming, tried to push her eyes to the back of her skull, and tried not to hear the horrible fluid sound that Patrick made as he told her to take his wallet and where to go. When she felt a hand touch her shoulder, her heart stopped, and so did her breathing.

All she could think about was escaping, running, but her legs wouldn't obey. They were caught or tied somehow, trapping her. Jerking away from the attacker, she tried to scream, only a raspy croak came from her throat. A second attempt was no better than the first.

"Whoa, Emma. It's me. It's Gabe. No one's trying to hurt you." Gabe sat down on the bed and tried to gather her into his arms, but she twisted away from him, evading his comfort and delivering a staggering elbow to his chest as she fought him in a blind panic. He finally settled for holding her wrists so she couldn't push him away or lash out at him with clenched fists.

When she was spent from the strain of trying to fight him, her long hair swung away from her face, and he could see that she had her eyes tightly closed, as if afraid of what she might see. In a small, terrified voice she pleaded, "Let me go. Please. I won't tell."

Gabe felt his jaw tighten and his chest constrict. Her resistance was nothing more than token at this point. The shock of his touch and the fear had drained her.

"Hey, it's me," Gabe assured her softly again, loosening his grip on her wrists. "I'm not trying to hurt you. You're tangled up in the sheet, Emma. That's all. It's Gabe. It's okay."

Gradually, as his words sank in, Emily stopped struggling. Like a flood, reality washed over her, and she opened her eyes. She was with Gabe, not in an Idaho farmhouse, but in Washington. Safe. For now.

This time when he drew her into his arms Emily didn't resist. One last shiver slid through her, and she wasn't sure if it was left over from the dream or created by the warmth of Gabe's touch as his hand rubbed her back in long strokes that seemed to travel the length of her nerves and back again.

The shirt beneath her cheek was soft and warm and familiar, an anchor she clung to while the dark images that lived in her dreams slowly faded. Her fingers curled and uncurled where they rested against his collarbones, the action an unconscious means of reassuring herself that Gabe was real. Suddenly aware of her position, Emily stiffened and shifted backward, appalled that she'd fallen into his arms twice in less than twelve hours. She wiped beneath her eyes to erase the tears that always came with the dream.

"What—" She cleared her throat. "What time is it?"

Gabe realized her query about the time was only an attempt to shift his attention away from her nightmare. "I think it's time to tell me about the bad guys."

Her hand stilled as she caught the satin binding of the blanket. A half-beat later she pulled it toward her, dropping it neatly across her hips to match the sheet she'd untangled. In the same tone that strangers used for meaningless party conversation, she asked, "What bad guys?"

"The ones in your dreams," he answered, his voice hard, unrelenting. "The ones who make you scream."

That finally got her full attention. She faced him with the panicked expression of a recovering alcoholic who'd been caught with one hand in the liquor cabinet and a mouth full of incriminating evidence.

"Who's after you, Emma?" he pressed.

She drew her legs up into a yogalike position, resting her hands in her lap. "It's an old nightmare. It comes back sometimes, usually when I'm in a strange place."

Although he wanted to, Gabe didn't call her a liar. Instead, he reached for her, the pressure on her arm forcing her upper body closer to where he sat on the edge of the bed. His shirt swallowed her small frame, the short sleeves falling below her elbow. Her hair rippled down her sides in loose waves.

"I had an old dream," she repeated, enunciating each word in a voice so compelling he was almost persuaded to believe her.

Gabe held on to her arm as if he could gauge the truth of her response by the warmth of her skin. "I have a lot of old dreams, and I don't wake up screaming."

"Then maybe we just react differently," she snapped.

"Yeah, we're different," Gabe allowed, but he wasn't talking about dreams.

Emma was silk, and he was flannel. She was elegant; he was common. She was hell-bent on running fast; he was determined to slow her down. He wanted to kiss her; the lady wouldn't like it.

Emma didn't want to swap spit or life stories. She wanted a new identity and nothing else. For some reason that made him angry. Too late he realized he'd never let go of her arm. They were too close; there was too much tension.

Then her gaze dropped nervously to his mouth, staring and darting away. He liked the way she looked all swallowed up in his shirt. And, God help him, he loved the way she kept looking at his mouth. Gabe leaned closer, his lips almost on hers.

Emily felt the heat between them. She didn't pull back or look away, but she didn't yield either. *Why didn't she just say no? Or draw back?*

Because the cold numbness inside her had begun to thaw. His fingers tunneled through her hair until he found skin. The pads of his fingers were rough and warm. The sensations he created made it difficult to think rationally.

While his fingers performed magic, she tried telling herself that her wires were crossed, that she was confusing a very understandable desire for a protector with the plain, old-fashioned sexual kind of desire. But common sense had deserted her light-years earlier. She was already contemplating how his mouth would feel against hers, how the stubble of beard would feel beneath her fingers and on her face.

The worst part of losing the battle with her common sense was that Gabe knew she'd lost. He was one step ahead of her, and he had been all night. He was so sure of himself. So sure of her. Pressure from his fingers adjusted her head a fraction, tilting it as he drew closer.

Just like the man, his kiss was a study in controlled intensity. His hand on her arm, his fingers against her neck, and his lips on hers, were the only points of contact between them, as if he wouldn't allow himself more. His tongue tasted her bottom lip, then swept up to lave the bow and traveled back again. He finessed her mouth open without her realizing what he was doing until it was too late. By then she'd already invited him in, and his tongue was twined with hers.

Gabe knew the exact moment Emma let go of her last reservation. He would have known even without the tiny sigh of surrender that caught in her throat. It was the same moment he discovered he was going to have to stop kissing her, because the kiss was more than he bargained for. He hadn't planned on the fire that caught hold of his soul as Emma welcomed him and his tongue slid home.

A minute earlier the kiss had seemed like a simple way to diffuse the sensual current that kept them warily circling each other. But his clever plan exploded on a soft sigh that spoke of need and uncertainty and unexpected passion. Maintaining any semblance of control once she'd surrendered was impossible. The sound of her sigh triggered a deeper need in him, one that wouldn't be satisfied with sampling the warm velvet sheath of her mouth. Unfortunately, it also triggered one of the few unbreakable commandments in his moral code—the one about taking advantage of women in trouble.

Reluctantly Gabe drew back, but when she leaned into him to prolong the kiss, he groaned a curse and almost relented. Until he noticed her eyes were still closed. That small symbol of trust stopped him cold.

Emma wasn't looking for sex; she was looking for a way to forget. Fear changed people, motivated them to grab hold of anything that made them feel alive. Taking her by the shoulders, he set her away from him as gently as he could and then dropped his hands.

A second later she surfaced and opened her eyes. Her parted lips were quickly pressed together, and her eyes widened with what he guessed was embarrassment as reality descended. Wrapping her arms around her midriff, she used body language to shut him out and put distance between them. She retreated into silence without giving him a clue as to what she was thinking. He was about ready to shake some words out of her when she finally spoke.

"I don't usually— Look, I don't want—"

"I know," he said curtly, unaccountably angry that she felt she had to explain.

Holding on to his temper, he got up, walked the few feet to the window, and leaned stiff-armed against the sash. He reminded himself that he had no right to nurse a bruised ego. His role in this mess was to be used and forgotten. A familiar role, and one he ought to be able to play in his sleep.

So why did her stammered rejection sting his pride so damned much?

Staring into the darkness outside, he said, "Let's just call what happened an icebreaker and forget it."

He felt rather than saw her jaw drop at his choice of words. Icebreaker was much too mild a term for what had transpired between them. After their kiss the only thing left of the ice was hot water, and they were in it.

"Excuse me!" she said from behind him, her voice tinged with indignation. "But an icebreaker is 'Do you think it's going to rain?' or 'Have you heard the one about the traveling salesman?'"

"Yeah, well, those are boring and overused," he said without turning.

"They're supposed to be. Who the hell gave you permission to substitute a kiss?"

"You did." He smiled into the night, knowing that his answer wouldn't sit well with Emma. It cut too close to the bone, but it was the truth.

Turning around, he tried to make out her expression. By design or accident her face was outside the path of light spilling from the bathroom. He put one hand in his jeans pocket and raked the other through his hair. Thanks to Patrick, he was walking a slippery tightrope in a pitch-black night without a net. Emma's nightmare changed his perspective on his role in this mess. He wasn't a baby-sitter; he was a bodyguard. At least until Patrick could ditch his assignment and get his ass back here to take over.

"Who the hell are you, Emma? And who's after you? The truth this time, and keep in mind that it's bad form to lie to a man who's willing to risk his life for you."

"I haven't asked you to risk your life," she pointed out stiffly. "Whatever you're doing, you're doing because you owe Patrick, not me."

"Dead is dead," Gabe informed her coldly. "It doesn't much matter who you died for or why." He walked back toward the bed. "Face some facts, darlin'. You can run, but you can't vanish in a puff of smoke with forty-eight cents. I'm flat broke myself, so we're going to have to build you a new set of paper the hard way, and it's going to take some time. Time means you stay here. As long as you're here, that puts me in the line of fire."

"No one knows I'm here except Patrick. I covered my tracks. No one can find me."

"You better hope so." He leaned down to make his next point, to make sure she heard every word. "*If* your nightmare finds you before you can disappear, he'll put"—Gabe made a gun out of his thumb and index finger and put it against her temple—"a bullet in your pretty little head." He paused, and then pulled the trigger. "*Bang!* And begging him won't save you."

Gabe waited for her to tell him that he was exaggerating. She didn't. He removed his hand and paced a few steps. The deep breath he took was audible in the quiet that had descended on the room like a pall.

"I hate it when I'm right," he quipped, but there was no humor in his comment. "But since I am, let me point out that right now the only thing between you and his bullet is me. So I'm sure you'll understand that I'd like to know a little more about the man pulling the trigger!"

For a long time Emily just stared at her hands, which were folded neatly in her lap. Her first impulse had been to tell him everything and ask him to take over since she needed all the help she could get. No matter how much she wanted to believe that she'd covered her tracks, the possibility existed that she hadn't. They found her at a government safe house. They could find her here.

As long as she stayed, his life was in danger. She didn't want to be responsible for anyone else's life.

Throwing off the covers, Emily slid out of bed. She flashed a fair amount of leg and probably a cheek before the back of the shirt drifted down. That was no big deal. Her skating costumes had shown as much or more.

"Thanks for the meal and the shower. But I'm not ready to play show-and-tell, so I'll get out of here. Out of your way. And then you won't be in danger."

Gabe had no intention of letting Emma walk out the door, even if he had to detain her bodily. "You're not going anywhere."

Emily faltered at the soft menace in his voice. He was a dark gray shadow by the window, a partially concealed predator daring his prey to make one wrong move, but she refused to be intimidated.

"Hide and watch, Gabriel. I've made it this far. I'll manage somehow."

"Your clothes are wet, and it's freezing outside." He noted the obvious excuses as if she were a simpleton who couldn't figure out how to use an electric clothes dryer or be trusted with sharp objects.

"Thanks for the weather report. I'll bundle up."

Emily found the kitchen light switch by trial and error while he watched from across the room. Simultaneously she flipped on the light and pulled up the washer lid. Despite his threat, he made no move to stop her, but she could feel his disapproval like a third presence in the room.

Frowning, Gabe watched Emma fish out the nun's habit and some scraps of red lace. This was the woman he'd seen only glimpses of, the one who took her whiskey neat and made no excuses. A good meal and a few hours of sleep before the nightmare had made her spirit immeasurably stronger. Of course almost anything would have been an improvement over the desperate woman who walked into his bar.

Emily tossed her underwear and the dress in the dryer as quickly as she could, and set the dial. "Polyester dries real fast. I ought to be out of your hair in about twenty minutes."

"I don't care how fast polyester or even silk underwear dries," he said as he joined her by the dryer. The red flannel shirt was unbuttoned and hung loose at his sides, the sleeves rolled up a couple of times. His T-shirt hinted at the hard muscles beneath it, and one hand was flattened against his abdomen. The turquoise ring and the silver chain bracelet were back on his hand and wrist.

"Emma, you're not going anywhere until I'm satisfied."

"Satisfied about what?" she demanded, trying not to stare at his chest but not wanting to risk eye contact either.

"That you can take care of yourself."

"I've done all right so far."

"Have you?" he asked with deadly calm. "Because it doesn't look like it from where I'm standing."

She glared up at him. "Then maybe you need to back off."

Big words for such a small lady, Gabe thought. Although sorely tempted, he didn't point out that she lacked the muscle to support her mouth. Nor did he mention that she was the one who'd come begging for help in the first place. Instead, he walked to the fridge and grabbed a two-liter Coke bottle. It was the closest thing to caffeine he could get his hands on at the moment, and he needed some time to think.

Without bothering to offer her any, he uncapped the soda, upended the plastic bottle, and chugged the cold liquid, relishing the carbonation burn as it slid down his throat. When he finished, he carefully screwed the cap back on. Still undecided about what to do, he put the soda away and closed the refrigerator. He leaned a forearm against the cool door, hooked an index finger in his front pocket, and studied her. She hadn't moved from her guard-dog position by the dryer.

"Nope," he said. "Distance didn't help a bit. I backed off and you still look like something Wart dragged in and spit out on the rug. Darlin', you're definitely on the pale side."

Stung by his criticism, she said, "People *expect* nuns to be pale."

"But you're not a nun, now, are you? And you're dead broke. Do you mind telling me how you plan to eat regular if you walk out that door with no credit cards and no money?"

"The same way everyone else does. I'll get a job."

"Got a résumé? References? Skills?"

Yeah, I have a million-dollar face, Emily thought, but managed not to say it out loud. Endorsement contracts weren't going to do her a bit of good when she stopped being Emily Quinn and became someone else.

"That's what I thought," Gabe said when she didn't answer. "No skills. Well, you didn't look like the handy type."

"And exactly what is the handy type?"

"Not you. You're too smooth, too cared for." He stared at her painted toes and ran his eyes slowly up the length of her legs.

Emily felt uncomfortable even though she'd been looked at by men for most of her life. Skimpy skating costumes left little to the imagination, and she'd gotten over being shy about her body a long time ago, but the way Gabe looked at her was different. It was personal. He wasn't looking at the skater, he was looking at her. Wherever his gaze lingered she felt warm, touched.

"When I thought you were a nun," he said, "the way you looked fooled me. I thought you had this delicate, nunlike quality about you. But that was before I got a good look at your body."

To her chagrin, she felt her nipples harden as his inspection stopped just below her shoulders. She clenched her teeth to keep from fidgeting. Good Lord! How could he do this to her from across the room?

"Emma darlin', you look like you've spent more time in the gym than you have on the job."

An indignant huff escaped her. He'd handed her a compliment and a complaint in the same breath. "I like to keep in shape."

He shifted to lean against the counter instead of the refrigerator and folded his arms. "Okay, so you work out. Have you ever worked?"

"Yeah, as a matter of fact, I have," she snapped. Ice skating was hard, grueling even. But his insinuation that she might be lazy wasn't the reason for her anger. Emily was angry because he could make her body respond without touching her, without asking her permission. Although she shouldn't be surprised. This was just one more area of her life over which she didn't have control.

"Maybe you've worked," he allowed. "But do you know what it's like to be the least important employee in the company? To clean toilets? Punch a clock? To have someone telling you what to do every minute? Because that's the only kind of job you can get without references."

Emily almost laughed, and a bitter smile lingered on her lips. Without realizing it, he'd stumbled on the two things she knew better than anything else—hard work and letting someone else run her life. She'd worked with blisters and bruises, sore tendons and muscle pulls. She'd worked twelve-hour days, seven days a week, fifty-two weeks a year. And every second she had someone telling her how she could do it better.

"Do you think you can do that, Emma?"

"Oh, I think I can manage. I've had people telling me when to breathe for twenty years." She resented his attitude, so much that she didn't stop to censor her words as she set him straight. "Punching a clock is no different from having to be at a rink at five in the morning, and I can't imagine a boss any harder to please than my coaches were."

"Coaches?" Gabe pushed away from the counter, suddenly interested. "Rink?"

Emily caught her breath at her mistake, and the sound of her distress only made her slip more glaring. She could see the wheels turning in Gabe's mind.

"Twenty years is more than a job," Gabe said slowly. "In the navy it's a career. You must have started young and been pretty good to have lasted so long at . . . skating, was it?"

"Excuse me." Like a coward, Emily headed for the bathroom and shut the door on his questions.

Left standing alone in the kitchen after Emma's vanishing act, Gabe resisted the urge to haul her out of the bathroom. Instead, he walked to the living room area and sank down in the chair that faced the bathroom. While he waited for Emma's reappearance, he searched his mind for the information he wanted.

The closest he got to sports was pool—eight ball, to be precise. Simple rules. One man, one stick, and sink the eight ball last. A simple game and one he understood, unlike ice skating, about which he didn't have a clue.

He shut his eyes and concentrated. The only names he had a prayer of remembering were Olympic gold medalists. If she hadn't won a gold, it was pretty hopeless. On the other hand, if she hadn't won a gold, she wouldn't be famo—

Gabe's eyes snapped open. Not Emma. *Emily. Emily Quinn.*

The only thing he could recall about her was that she had a bunch of world championships and had never won an Olympic gold medal. "Always a bridesmaid, never a bride" was how Skeeter Daniel put it.

Some sailors chose *Playboy* models, but not Skeeter. He was an odd little fellow from Minnesota—an expert marksman and jumper who had a real talent for blowing up things. He followed ice skating in general, and Emily Quinn in particular. Thank God for Skeeter, Gabe thought, otherwise he never would have matched Emily Quinn with Emma's face.

And if he figured it out, then someone else sure as hell would, he reminded himself grimly. Even in a tiny speck of a town like this one. *They might have already.*

Dredging up memories, he tried to compare the woman in his bathroom with Emily-the-Ice-Princess. He remembered looking at the cover of a *Sports Illustrated* that Skeeter had lying around, but there wasn't the connection to her that he felt tonight.

Because she didn't need you then.

As much as he hated it, being needed was a drug to him, an addiction that had been nurtured by repetition over the years. He was addicted to the instant connection forged between people in crisis. Even though he knew all too well that the bond would fade, and he'd be forgotten once the crisis was over.

Somehow, explaining away his attraction to Emma as a conditioned response felt safer than admitting the woman got to him on a more basic level.

While Gabe sat waiting, dawn came sneaking into the room like a coward. Gabe hated dawn and dusk. Too many shades of gray. He liked his world black or white. That's what bothered him about Emma. She had too many shades of gray.

When his bathroom door finally opened, Emma walked into the room wearing the pair of jogging pants he had hanging on the back of the door. They puddled on top of her feet and she held the edge of the waist as if she weren't sure the drawstring was tight enough. She didn't look like much of a threat to anyone. *What on earth have you done to get yourself into this mess, Emma?*

"I was cold." She tugged on the pants. "Hope you don't mind."

He tilted his head toward the other chair. "I mind a lot. But not about the pants. Take a load off, *Miss Quinn.* Or should that be Mrs.?"

She blanched at the sound of her last name, but sat down. "No."

"Good." Gabe leaned up in the chair and braced his elbows on his knees. He clasped his hands together and gave her a look that brooked no refusal. He was done playing games. "Tell me."

FIVE

"Where do you want me to start?" Emily asked.

"Let's start with how you know Patrick."

She tried not to tense up, but he began with the question she was least prepared to answer. She forced herself to meet his gaze and not look away while she told as much of the truth as possible. "He was assigned to me for a while."

"You're a witness." It was a statement, not a question. He could have been conducting a military debriefing for all the emotion he showed in his face.

"Not anymore."

"But you were."

"Yeah. I was in the wrong place at the wrong time. I'm in this mess because I saw a man put a gun in a trash can."

"Explain."

"It's like corroborating evidence. I didn't see him pull the trigger, but I can place him at the scene with the murder weapon in his hand. Afterward the marshals said it was one in a million. The hit man had one of those plastic guns you can get through X ray. The marshals told me the hit was supposed to be done in the men's room; seems the victim *always* made a detour into the bathroom before boarding a plane."

"But this time he didn't make that pit stop."

"No, he went straight to the gate and sat off in a corner. And that's where he quietly died, with his baseball cap pulled over his eyes like he was trying to sleep."

"I assume the hit man used a silencer?"

"They said so. I didn't hear the shot. I looked up and saw a man put what looked like a gun in the trash can. It took a couple of seconds to register. Someone hollered that a guy had been shot and then it clicked. I yelled, 'He did it! He had a gun!' in the middle of the Los Angeles airport.

"Everyone hit the deck when they heard 'gun,' but some young Nebraska-corn-fed security giant with more guts than brains was standing right next to him when I pointed. He tackled the guy, wrestled him to the ground, and sat on him. Between the two of us, we managed to blunder our way into apprehending a bona fide wiseguy—Joseph Bookman. It was one of those freak accidents. A split second in time."

He pondered that for a moment, made calculations in his head, and asked, "When was this?"

"Three months ago."

"This wouldn't have gone to trial already."

"No." She shifted uneasily in her chair. She knew where he was going with this.

"That means you haven't testified yet, Emma."

"I'm not going to testify. I'm not cooperating any longer."

"It doesn't work that way. You don't just 'decide' not to cooperate."

Emily bit her tongue on the truth and told a half-truth in its place. "The price for their protection is too high. They want me to have plastic surgery to change my face."

Expelling a displeased breath, Gabe said, "Silly me. I was hoping I had exaggerated your celebrity."

Shaking her head, she said, "The commercial started about three months ago. The marshals said in five years it might not be a problem, but right now they wouldn't guarantee my safety unless I had the surgery."

"Whoa. Go back. What commercial?"

"I forgot. You're the man who doesn't open his newspapers and doesn't have a television." Emily paused. "You don't even have one in the bar?"

"Nope. Wasn't one there when I bought the place. No money for it since then."

"Well, if you had one, you'd have seen the commercial for the mascara—it's a great close-up of this face—and you'd also know that for the last year every sports program and news tabloid wanted to relive the end of my career. They explained in excruciating detail their version of why I never got the gold medal. If I didn't give them a story or if they thought my story was too dull, they made one up.

"For the record, I didn't retire because of a nervous breakdown after my parents' death. I didn't retire because my coach was sexually harassing me. I didn't retire because I was too old. I am not bulimic, have not had a sex change, and I did not retire to have Elvis's baby."

Gabe had to fight a smile. "Was it really that bad?"

"Close." He detected a hint of sadness in her voice as she continued. "Most of them went with the sympathy angle on my parents' death. Hank and Rosalie were older than you'd think. I didn't come along until they had retired from skating and performing. They went in their sleep, one right after the other."

She pulled up her pants leg and pointed out the fading surgery scars.

"Car accident. The real truth behind my retirement is that the ankle just never healed. It's the nerve damage. I can't feel the ice well enough to take off or land the jumps anymore. Emily Quinn, the American ice princess, retired because her foot won't do what she tells it to sometimes." She shrugged. "But Emily still has a really high recognition rating with the average television viewer and a whole fistful of endorsement contracts."

She let the fleece material drop back down over her ankle and drew her legs up. Wrapping her arms around them, she stared down at nothing in particular. "Before my retirement there was the shock of my parents' unexpected death. That made the news because we were supposed to be the founding of a dynasty. They were pairs skaters—silver medalists—which is pretty damn good for an American pair. They were supposed to be around when I brought home the gold. There's another Kodak moment shot to hell."

Looking up at him, she said, "I've decided that instant camera moments are good only for reminding us of what is gone and will never come again."

"Pretty cynical."

"Blame it on the year. It's been a nail-biter from day one. Before my parents died, there was the car accident that screwed up my ankle."

"And then you ended up in the wrong place at the wrong time."

"Yeah, I finally had financial security and no place to be at five in the morning. And then I cause the arrest of a very nasty man whose associates would like to see me dead."

"So, why not change your face and start over? The endorsement contracts? Do you need the money?"

She got quiet, and unfolded her legs as Wart meowed and jumped onto the arm of her chair. He straddled it like a doily with his legs dangling lifelessly over each side. She stroked him behind the ears for a minute and then said, "No."

"So, why?" he pressured her.

Emily looked up from the cat and met his gaze. "I don't want to change my face because it's the only thing I have left that's truly mine. The only family album I have, the only momento of the past, is the one I see when I look in the mirror."

Emotions Gabe didn't want to face welled up inside him. His mirror had been his family album for a long time too. He wasn't sure which was worse—having your security ripped away when you were six or having your world explode when you were grown. Dealing with Emma objectively was difficult enough without empathy getting in the way and sidetracking him.

Unable to sit still any longer, Gabe stood up, hoping physical action could help him shake off even older, less charming memories that threatened to surface. He grabbed some wood to replenish the stove and shoved it in harder than necessary. While he worked at rebuilding the fire, he kept after the part of her story that bothered him.

"Why not cut your hair or color it? Or both? Why not use colored contact lenses? When there were so many other options, why would the government let you walk away?"

The door of the cast iron wood stove clanked shut as he swung around to face her and answered his own question. "They wouldn't. Which means Patrick's career is on the line because he let you walk away." She saw something like guilt shadow Gabe's expression, but it turned to anger too quickly to be sure. "You kiss him too, Emma? Did you make him promises with that body of yours to get what you wanted?"

"It wasn't like that." Emily couldn't stand the way he was looking at her, as if she'd done something terrible. *Which she had.* Shaking off the memories, she got up, inexplicably drawn to the pool table. "You don't understand. We were close, that's all."

"Darlin'," he whispered, joining her by the table and leaning close to her ear, "you don't have to tell me how close . . . how *intimate* two people can get if they're thrown into a dangerous situation. I think I had that all figured out when you kissed me. I just want to know if you kissed Patrick."

When he pulled back, her shoulders did a little dance as a shiver hit her unexpectedly. She brushed the backs of her fingers across her ear, trying to rub away an unsettling sensation left by the feel of his breath and lips against her skin. "I didn't kiss Patrick." She leveled a cold gaze at him. "And I didn't kiss you."

"I could have sworn that was a kiss."

Narrowing her eyes, Emily warned him not to push it. "That kiss was your idea, not mine. You listen carefully, because I'm going to say this only one last time. Patrick was my friend. Nothing more."

When she pushed away from the pool table, Gabe stopped her with a question, all the teasing gone from his voice. "Then why did he give you the dog tag?"

"He was reassigned," Emily lied, forcing out the words as they stuck in her throat. She spun the pretty web of half-truths she'd rehearsed in the bathroom. "But he knew how afraid and alone I was, so when he . . . when he found out he wouldn't be around to protect me anymore, he gave me the dog tag and told me where I could find you if I needed someone."

"Let me get this straight." Gabe drew her closer, locking his gaze with hers. "He gave you the dog tag because he got pulled off your detail for this other assignment? Sort of like insurance to make you feel better until he got back?"

"Yeah, that's why he gave it to me. Just in case something went wrong."

Oh, hell, thought Gabe as he leaned back on the edge of the pool table, suddenly tired. This was finally beginning to make a wicked sort of sense. And none of it good news.

His buddy had parted with the tag so easily because he never thought Emily would actually use it! Good old

Patrick loved grand gestures. Probably figured he'd get the dog tag back soon enough with no harm done, and look like a fine fellow in the process. Only something bad happened in the meantime, and now Gabe was left to pick up the pieces until Patrick surfaced.

"So, what went wrong, Emma?"

"No. You can't have it. My finger is still on the card. I've changed my mind." Emily pleaded desperately with Patrick, who answered with a sinful grin and a shake of his head.

"Baby, as soon as it touched the discard stack, it belonged to me."

He didn't give her any breaks. Not when they played cards. He played cut-throat gin for a penny a point. So far she owed him twenty-three dollars and seventy-one cents.

"Fine." She let go of the card and motioned for him to take it. "I'm going to beat you in a second or two anyway."

"Now, there's an empty threat if I ever heard one." He perused his cards. "Unless you got Danny-boy peeking at my cards through the window and giving you hand signals." He grabbed his radio even though no one could possibly see through the drawn shades. "Dano, are you working for the enemy? You telling this woman about my cards?"

The silence erased all Patrick's good-natured humor. He keyed the radio again. . . .

"What went wrong?" Gabe repeated, forcing her to look at him.

Emily knew the answer to that question would be the biggest lie of all. What made the lies worse for her was that she'd somehow ended up standing in Gabe's arms, in the cradle of his thighs. She was drawing the strength to lie *to* him *from* him. Her clasped hands were centered on his chest, as if this were the most natural posture for a conversation between strangers.

But she didn't pull back. If she had to relive that night, she couldn't think of a better place to do it than in the safety of Gabe's arms. She forced herself to tell as much of the truth as possible, changing the names and omitting her last conversation with Patrick—the one about finding Gabe. Even as she told the carefully edited version, the original played in her mind in living color. Just as real as it had been four days before.

As the story unraveled, Gabe's mind reeled with the implication of what she said. Two deputy marshals had been killed, but that wasn't the worst of it. A *marshal* had been involved in the attempt on Emma's life. Some very angry, very clever, very connected people wanted her dead.

Getting rid of the witness would keep Bookman from making a deal with the feds. Emma was the first domino in a chain that could bring down some heavy duty crime figures. Everybody would be coming after her. The marshals and the bad guys.

No matter how cleverly she thought she'd covered her tracks, she was an amateur. They'd be coming. The only question was how long before they got here, and if he'd be ready for them.

Thank God he'd routed that damned fax through New York. That would buy him some time if the feds got suspicious about the letter, a week at least. Patrick should be in contact long before then. Maybe between the two of them they could sort through this mess. In the meantime he'd have to make plans to get Emma out.

Unfortunately she was in no condition emotionally to go anywhere. She needed some time to deal with everything that had happened, and he wasn't sure he could give her time.

He heard not only the terror in her voice, but also the guilt at leaving an officer she barely knew to die. Underlining it all was a courage she would never recognize. But the truth was only pure guts had gotten her this far.

"I couldn't stay," she told him, apologizing to him again for failing—almost as if she'd failed him personally. "I couldn't stay. I tried. I did. I'm so sorry. I picked up the gun, but I couldn't do it, and there was so much blood, and—"

"And it's all right," Gabe told her softly as she struggled with the guilt. He could see it in her eyes.

Emma fought so hard for control, but the price was just as high as letting go of the emotions. He understood where all the tears in the bar had come from last night. She'd been saving them up, afraid to shed them until she was safe.

"You don't need to justify anything. You did the best you could, darlin'. The best anyone could have."

"No!" A tear fought past her defenses and slid into the corner of her mouth. Her tongue wiped it off instantly, erasing it as if she had no right to cry. Her knuckles were white and her hands clenched so hard, the pressure dug them into his chest. "No, what I did was leave the man who saved my life alone to die."

"Emma." He shook her gently by the shoulders. "He knew the risk when he took the job."

"Did he know that I'd take his keys, and get in *his* car, and drive away while he lay on the floor and quietly bled to death on cheap beige carpeting? In the dark, with no one to hold his hand or close his eyes?" She looked up at him, regret written all over her face and unshed tears glittering in her eyes, but she was angry too. Her hands had curled into fists clutching his T-shirt. "Do you think he knew *that* when he signed on?"

"I think he knows he did a damn good job. You're still alive, and as far as I'm concerned, that's all that matters."

"Is it?" she asked softly, full of doubt, tears streaking down her cheeks one after the other. Slowly she let go of his shirt and smoothed the wrinkles from the fabric.

The uncertainty of the question and the pain in her eyes ripped Gabe's own control away. He cupped her face, using his thumbs to brush off the dampness on her cheekbones. "You tell me."

His mouth captured hers, absorbing the salty moistness left from her tears. Without waiting for an invitation this time, he slid his tongue inside, deepening the caress, seducing a response. This was a hot, hard kiss that spoke of sex and life. He told himself it was only an expedient way to remind her how it felt to be alive, to shock her into realizing why life was so important, something precious and never questioned.

But half a heartbeat after her tongue touched his, the kiss became more than a lesson in life. He'd never been very good at expressing his feelings with words. His whole life had been show not tell. So he used his mouth and his hands to show Emma that she was safe, cared for, and alive. In the process, he lost himself in the feel of her body against his as her hands crept around his neck and her breasts pressed softly against him.

Emily couldn't think anymore. Not with his mouth hard against hers and his hands tracing the curve of her spine to the small of her back. The world stumbled, regrouped, and went on without her, leaving her in an unfamiliar place filled with sensations that almost scared her in their intensity.

He ran his hands past the curve of her hips and pulled her up to meet his arousal. Her muscles tightened and naturally arched her pelvis into his. She wanted the contact, the feel of his body against hers. She needed it. Suddenly nothing else mattered except the pulse between her legs that grew stronger each time he teased her by thrusting his tongue into her mouth in long, hard strokes.

When he slowly brought his palms back up, his fingers dragged up the edge of the shirttail, giving him access to her bare skin. At first he only smoothed his hands along her sides. Then he toyed with the loose waistband of the jogging pants by sliding his fingers inside the edge and rubbing circles at the small of her back.

Gabe knew there would be no panties to hinder him if he let his hand dip lower. He'd feel the sweet softness of her cheek in his palm. All he had to do was fill his hand. He groaned when she caught and sucked shyly on his tongue, doing to him what he'd been doing to her— previewing an intimacy that went far beyond kissing.

His hands shifted to bracket her midriff as he broke the kiss and trailed his lips down the column of her neck. Her skin was hot beneath his mouth and hands as he pushed her breasts up, accepting their weight and cupping them. Her fingers dug into his shoulders as his mouth found one nipple through the textured cotton shirt and sucked. Emma's reaction was an audible gasp and ragged sigh. And a soft word that might have been "please" made his arousal throb in answer.

That was the moment Gabe began to think of stripping her and lifting her up to the pool table. The bed was only four strides away, but that was too damn far. He was hard and the only thing on his mind was burying himself inside Emma.

And that was the moment Marsha Jean Petit banged on the door at the bottom of the stairs. "Gabe! You home?" she hollered. "The bar's a wreck! I told you I should have stayed. What happened to the window?"

Gabe would have ignored Marsha Jean if he hadn't given her a *complete* set of keys to the bar, including the one for the apartment door. With a frustrated groan he dropped his hands and found Emma's mouth for one more quick kiss before she pulled away completely. God, she was made to be kissed. Right now her eyes still glittered from interrupted passion. Her lips were swollen, especially the bottom one, and the stubble of his beard had reddened the edge of her mouth.

Rubbing his chin, he decided he was going to have to shave today. He also decided that if she didn't close that mouth, he was going to have to close it for her with another kiss. Unfortunately he had only three seconds left before Marsha Jean unlocked the door and started up the stairs. So Gabe put a finger across Emma's lips and finished the conversation they'd been having before he kissed her.

"Darlin', that's what being alive feels like. The next time you're not sure whether being alive is all that matters, you think again. Because it's the only thing between you and an eternity of nothing."

She didn't argue. Right now she couldn't form a complete sentence, much less debate philosophy.

"Gabe!" Marsha Jean's southern accent boomed up the stairwell. "I let myself in. You decent?"

If Marsha Jean hadn't been the sole support of two innocent children, Gabe would have cursed her. Instead, without taking his gaze off of Emma, he hollered back, "As decent as I'm going to get. Come on up."

You will anyway, he added silently.

Emily saw her chance and retreated across the room, ostensibly to check on her clothes in the dryer. In reality she simply wanted to put as much distance between her hormones and Christian Gabriel as possible. The man was deadly all right, and she had no intention of presenting an easy target. To him that kiss was simply a way of proving his point—a way to win.

He probably didn't have the faintest idea what he did to her on the inside, and she wanted to keep it that way. She wanted no regrets when she walked out his front door with a brand-new identity. And she didn't want emotions getting in the way of the secret she kept. She didn't need any more guilt.

"I was worried about you," Marsha Jean said as she crossed the threshold carrying a casserole dish in one hand and a wooden baseball bat in the other. She had on a serviceable but worn down-filled coat with a cinched waist and big pockets. "I saw you holding your ribcage last night. How are you?"

"I've been better."

"I can see that," she agreed, casting an eye over him and the clothes that had obviously been slept in. "Is your razor broke, or are you planning on growing that beard out?"

"As a matter of fact, I was just thinking about shaving."

"Thinking. That'd be a novel idea for you." She held out the baseball bat. "I told little Jeffie that you got into another fight, and he said to give you this to use until spring training."

Gabe grinned as he visualized her son Jeffie, who was an eight-year-old towhead but older than Job emotionally. He'd been the man of the family for too many years already. Gabe accepted the bat and gave it a mock swing. "Nice one."

"He's gotta have it back by March the twenty-first." Marsha Jean giggled. "God, love him. He's convinced that major league scouts come to Little League games, and they won't take him seriously if he uses his old aluminum bat."

"I can see his point," Gabe said with a grin as he laid the bat on the pool table behind him. "Thank him for me. I'll take really good care of it."

"You better or there'll be hell to pay. I gotta tell you—hell hath no fury like Jeffie in a snit," she warned him ominously, and then changed the subject by holding up the covered dish. "Couldn't sleep last night, so I made casseroles for everyone. Here's yours. The kids call it Egg-o-rama. It's really sort of a quiche thing instead of a casserole. And before you start getting all macho on me, let me just tell you that real men *do* eat quiche because they aren't afraid of anything except a good woman. And judging from your love life lately, you've got to be a real man. A good woman scares the hell out of you."

Without waiting for an invitation, Marsha Jean made a beeline for the kitchen. Or attempted to until she caught sight of Emily standing quietly by the dryer. If the waitress had been a car, she'd have left skid marks on the floor. As she stopped, the ceramic dish lid clattered and threatened to fly off before she grabbed it.

"Sister!"

"Hello," Emily said, wishing she had the glasses she'd left by the bed. Fortunately, even without them Marsha Jean had made the connection between her face and last night's nun instead of the connection to Emily Quinn.

Marsha Jean's eyes widened at the implication of finding a nun out of uniform in the apartment of a single heterosexual male. In rapid succession she noted the rumpled bed, Emily's unbound hair, and her general appearance of having just been kissed hard. A second later Marsha Jean's mouth hung open as she stared at the front of Emily's shirt.

Hesitantly Emily dropped her gaze and then shut her eyes in embarrassment. There was a noticeable circle of moisture where Gabe had sucked her nipple through the shirt. It was too odd a place for her to have spilled anything, and the circle was just about the perfect size to match her aureole.

SIX

"Excuse me," Marsha Jean said abruptly, and dumped the casserole on the coffee table. "Gabe, a word please."

Emily shot a stricken glance at him, not sure whether Marsha Jean was jealous or offended. Or both. Either way, she had to be pacified, and Gabe had to do the pacifying.

He didn't appear the least bit uncomfortable or anxious as Marsha Jean advanced on him purposely. He certainly didn't act like he'd been caught red-handed with another woman, and that fact inexplicably pleased Emily. Despite her intention to stay clear of Gabe emotionally, she was much happier with the idea that the blond waitress was a platonic friend rather than Gabe's lover.

This is a classic Patrick Talbot moment, Gabe thought as he waited for what he assumed would be a very large piece of his waitress's mind. She was obviously outraged at the thought of her sainted boss deflowering a nun. Marsha Jean was slender but tall, so Gabe didn't have to lean over very far when she grabbed his arm and hauled him close enough to whisper.

"Have you completely lost your mind?" Marsha Jean hissed, her face only inches from his. "I know I told you that you needed to get back in the saddle, but she's a *nun*, for God's sake. Haven't you got a shred of decency in that thick head of yours? You've . . . you've . . ."

Words seemed to fail her, and she looked back over her shoulder at Emma for inspiration. Obviously finding it in Emma's anxious expression, she whipped back around to continue her tirade. Her grip on his arm tightened with every word. "Don't you know what you've done? You've *seduced*—"

This time words didn't fail her; they were ripped away by the startling revelation Gabe could see written all over her stunned face. Marsha Jean dropped his arm and turned around very slowly, as if uncertain of what she might see. She stared for a long time before she croaked, "Oh, my God. You're Emily Quinn."

"Well, I guess we can skip the introductions," Gabe noted.

Over the top of Marsha Jean's head, Emma and Gabe stared at each other, wordlessly trying to agree on who would handle the situation. Gabe finally nodded his head as an indication that he'd do the honors if and when Marsha Jean shut up.

"Emily Quinn," the waitress repeated. "I can't believe this. Annabelle is just going to die! You are my little girl's idol. She was heartbroken when you weren't in the Olympics, until she figured out that America would need a new princess. So I got her these cute little skates when her birthday rolled around. I got a pair too. Now every Saturday morning I have to take her over to the rink in Marysville or out to Sutter's Pond. The weather's been so cold this past month that it's frozen solid. The pond's not very big, but then, neither is she. She's only—"

Marsha Jean stopped and groped behind her with her hand until she made contact with Gabe's chest. "Stop me, please. I'm rambling."

"I'm not stepping in front of that train," he said dryly, and disengaged his T-shirt from her grasp. "But since you've put the brakes on yourself, take off your coat, Marsha Jean. Now that you've barged in, I think we could use your help."

"W-wait," Emily stammered hurriedly, and glared at Gabe, doing her best to insinuate that he'd taken leave of his senses. Whatever his plan was, she didn't like it. She didn't want to be responsible for anyone else getting hurt. Besides that, Marsha Jean didn't look like the kind of woman who could keep a secret. "I don't know if that's such a good idea. We shouldn't involve her. It's not—"

"Oh, but I want to be involved. Besides, it's too late to close the barn door! The horses have already made a run for it," Marsha Jean told her, and crossed her arms. Plastic explosives weren't going to budge her until she got the whole story. Addressing Gabe, the waitress said, "So, tell me. What zany plot have you two cooked up to keep your affair out of the press? We are talking about an affair, aren't we? It'll just break my heart if we aren't!"

Gabe grinned and lied with an ease that amazed Emily. "As a matter of fact, we were discussing the possibility of an affair when you walked in."

"*What?*" Emily asked, regretting her decision to let him handle this. Her fingers itched to choke him. "As I recall, it wasn't a discussion! You were doing most of the *talking.*"

"No." Gabe appeared to ponder for a minute. "As I recall, you opened your mouth as much as I did."

Emily gasped at his less-than-subtle innuendo. Marsha Jean laughed so hard, she had to clamp a hand over her mouth.

"Oh, now, don't be shy," Marsha Jean chided when she recovered. With a wave of her hand she marched into the kitchen and started looking through the cabinets for plates. "And don't be stingy," she said, still chuckling a little. "This is as close as I'll get to an affair until my kids are grown. At least let me live vicariously through the two of you."

"We can trust her," Gabe told Emma as he came to stand beside her. The beginning of a plan was taking shape. "And we need her. Besides, she can cook."

"What's that supposed to mean?" Emily whispered irritably. "If she's such a good cook, then have the affair with her!"

"Jealous, darlin'?" Gabe quipped, and suffered an elbow to his bruised ribs.

Marsha Jean overheard. "Oh, honey, don't worry about me. I'd have to kill that man before dessert. He has way too much testosterone for me, and I chatter way too much for him." She stopped setting out plates on the coffee table and looked at Emily with speculation.

"You now, you're quiet. You listen more than you talk. And that's what Gabe needs."

"What Gabe *needs* is a good—"

Interrupting her, Marsha Jean ordered, "Now, now! Come have some breakfast. I bet you two were so busy throwing caution to the four winds and discussing all that important stuff that you forgot to eat." She giggled. "Emily, you can kick Gabe's butt after breakfast. I'll help."

In spite of herself, Emily had to laugh. It was impossible to stay irritated with Marsha Jean. She was a force of nature, a whirlwind that whipped everyone in her path into shape. And it was so nice to be normal again, at least for a little while.

"So, what happened to the window?" the blonde asked as they sat down.

A half hour later Emily and Gabe had eaten most of the casserole for breakfast. Marsha Jean had sided enthusiastically with Gabe on just about every issue of how Emily Quinn was going to be made over into someone new. The waitress swore it would be easy to fool those pesky reporters on the trail of celebrity romance. Despite Emily's protest that nothing was really settled, the woman was on the phone to her baby-sitter to arrange for an extra few hours.

When she hung up, Marsha Jean gathered up her coat and keys. "Listen, Gabe, Sunday school is about to start. I gotta go raid the church's garage sale closet for some clothes while the doors are unlocked, but I'll be back in half an hour to pick up Emily. I should have everything else we need at home."

"She'll be ready," Gabe answered without consulting Emily.

Forcing herself to hold her tongue until the waitress was down the steps, Emily gathered up the dishes and took them to the kitchen. She felt like a spectator in her own life. All the decisions were being made by people she barely knew. Of course, that wasn't a whole lot different from how her life as a skater had been. She'd been expected to show up, wear the clothes they gave her, do as she was told, and keep her mouth shut. Gabe expected her to do the same. He expected her to give him control, and that made her·angry.

She reopened the argument the moment she heard the stairwell door close. Flinging the dish towel back to the cabinet, she said, "Now that Marsha Jean is gone, maybe I can squeeze a word in! Gabe, I don't think you've given this makeover enough thought. The nun's habit was fine. It got me here in one piece. You know it works. Why change now? Marsha Jean didn't recognize me in it!"

"Yes, she did."

"*Not* while I was wearing it!"

"Emma, we've been through this. You aren't listening. We do not want you to attract attention. In this town you will get more attention as a nun than as my mousy little cousin from Indiana." He got up and went to his closet. "We don't get too many nuns around here. Trust me."

"Trust you? Ha! That's what the government said, and look where that got me!"

"Well, you're not trusting the government anymore," he told her as he pulled clothes off hangers. "You're trusting me."

"Only because I'm desperate."

"Thank you. That's my point exactly about the makeover. You don't have a choice."

"I don't think a change of disguise is necessary yet." Emma knew her objection was repetitive and weak even as she made it. Despite the urgency, she wasn't sure she was ready to give up her old self and plunge into the new.

Gabe sighed. "Look, darlin', I know you and that habit have been through the war together, and it's your security blanket, but this makeover is going to have to happen sometime. You can't skulk around up here forever."

"Wouldn't it be better if I just stayed out of sight rather than risk being recognized?"

"No. It's better if you try out your new look *here*, where there's less chance of your being recognized. Besides, I've got to take care of some business. It'll be easier if you can go with me. After what you told me this morning, I don't like the idea of leaving you alone."

"Go with you where?"

"Cemeteries, for a start."

"Not much chance of being recognized there," she pointed out in case he missed the obvious. "Everyone's dead!"

"You've made my point again." Gabe smiled. "I need to find the name of someone deceased who would have been about your age but died young. Then I'll need to check the social security records to make sure they were never issued a card."

"That won't take long. I can stay here. And you do all the social security stuff by computer from here. I thought you could just hack in or something."

"Look, the cemetery isn't the only problem. We still have to send off for the duplicate birth certificate, which could take a week even if we rush it, and we don't want to do that. Calls too much attention to us." He rummaged through some drawers and pulled out what looked suspiciously like black briefs. "I can't have a nun hanging around the bar for the amount of time it takes to do all this."

Gabe walked into the bathroom. "I'm taking a shower," he announced. "Stop worrying. Marsha Jean used to be a shampoo girl. I'm sure she'll do a great job. Besides, the best place to hide is in plain sight," he said before shutting the door.

"In plain sight," Emily murmured to the closed door. "Well, you're not the target, Mr. Gabriel. Or the guinea pig."

But he was a target now. As much of a target as she was.

They were sitting ducks waiting for the opening day of hunting season. Only no one would tell them when that day was coming.

The Rock Falls police station was an old brick building dressed up with a new coat of white paint and fancy gold lettering on the plate glass door. The station didn't do a booming business any day of the week, but Sundays were especially slow. At least that's what Gabe decided as he strode through the front door. The dispatcher was involved in an obviously personal call, but Officer Derick Willis was giving the city value for their tax dollars. He always did.

A scraggly mustache and sideburns that would have made Elvis proud did their best to cover up Willis's baby face, but he couldn't do much about his small, wiry build or his age. He was young, maybe early twenties, and new to the force. But what he lacked in impressive physical stature and experience he made up for in determination and shrewdness. Gabe imagined Willis just might be police chief one day if he wasn't lured away by a bigger city. All the more reason to be careful, he cautioned himself.

Willis stood the moment he spotted Gabe, and offered his hand. Gabe doubted the boy's gun had ever cleared leather in the line of duty, or that it ever would. But he suspected Willis kept himself ready all the same, that an examination of his targets at the range would show tightly grouped shots. The boy took his duty seriously, too seriously. Last month he had actually given someone a jaywalking ticket.

Ordinarily, a guy like Willis would have set Gabe's teeth on edge. But he was also the first one to open his wallet when a family was in trouble. He did odd jobs for the seventy-year-old widow who lived next door to the station and had an 8 GALLON DONOR sticker from the Darrington blood bank on his car.

"Hey, Gabriel. What can I do you for?"

Gabe shook his hand. "Someone threw a rock through my bar window last night."

With a what-are-things-coming-to kind of sigh,

Willis pointed to a chair beside his desk. Then he tsk-tsked and said, "Better file a report on that. You're going to need one anyway for your insurance in case they come back and do more damage. Never hurts to get your ducks in a row."

For the next ten minutes Willis asked a number of questions and hunted-and-pecked his way through an incident report. When he finished, he snatched it out of the typewriter and slapped it on the desk with a pen. "You look that over and sign it. I'll get us some coffee. Black, right?"

Gabe nodded and smiled when the officer turned away. Coffee equaled a bribe for staying awhile longer, for shooting the breeze and relieving the boredom. Choking down a bad cup of coffee was a small price to pay for information.

Willis liked to talk about the job and the latest in law enforcement toys. But Rock Falls was a small, peaceful town without much in the way of real crime beyond petty theft and the occasional bar fight. Most of the other cops were happy with the low crime rate and carried old-fashioned six-shot revolvers. Willis saw Gabe as an oasis in a desert of unbelievers. Gabe liked toys, guns, and ammo.

When Willis came back, Gabe accepted the coffee and let him drone on for a while before casually saying, "You know, hearing you talk makes me miss the action. Makes me miss the rush of getting orders."

Willis's eyes widened in surprise. "Didn't think you missed anything. Thought you said you were glad to be out."

"Oh, I am. But I miss the rush. You know the one I'm talking about, don't you? The charge you get when you know something might be going down for your team. You swallow your fear and grab your gear."

Leaning back in his chair, Willis dangled his empty mug from his index finger and nodded sagely. "Oh, yeah. Yeah. I know just what you mean. A rush like that puts the fear of God in you and starts the heart pump."

"Anything juicy lately?" Gabe asked, studying the officer's reaction without appearing to care. "Any dangerous fugitives we citizens should be looking out for? Any mad killers on the loose?"

"Nah. No such luck. Nothing that'd even make a good story for one of those tabloid 'news' shows," Willis scoffed.

"Can't be that dull around here," Gabe insisted. "Those people can fabricate a story out of just about anything."

"They couldn't from the stuff I'm getting lately. A couple of prisoners escaped from county during transport to their robbery hearing, but that's about it in the fugitive department. Unless you count our regular hit parade." He pointed to the wall behind him. Posters of law enforcement's most wanted were thumbtacked to the wall.

"Doubt you'll see any of those gentlemen in Rock Falls." Gabe put his cup down, laying the groundwork for his departure.

"Don't I know it. I got a buddy—a county badge down in northern California—he just hit pay dirt."

Gabe forgot about leaving, glued to the chair by the

way Willis looked over at the dispatcher to make sure he was still on the phone. "How's that?"

"This is not for public circulation, but my buddy just had to drop a dime to rub it in." Willis gave him a shrug and a sore-loser smile. "He's the one that found the abandoned car. Seems the feds have misplaced a mighty important person. A smooth professional by the name of Joseph Bookman. Just disappeared during a routine prisoner transfer yesterday. The deputy marshal disappeared with him. Every badge in three counties is making like a bloodhound on this one. And coming up with zip so far."

Carefully schooling his features to shield his reaction from Willis, Gabe realized that Willis didn't know the half of it. Gabe bit back a curse. The situation just kept getting worse. Any lingering doubts he had about Emma's story evaporated. Given what he knew, he had to wonder if the missing marshal was dead-never-to-be-found or if the son of a bitch was the same one who'd come after Emma, the one who was working both sides of the fence. That was a question he couldn't ask and Willis couldn't possibly answer.

"We don't take it well when one of our own goes down or missing," Gabe said, including himself in the universal fraternity of men who served their country with a gun.

"No, we don't." Willis leaned back in his chair and laced his fingers to make a rest for his head. "But there's not much chance of that around here. We're not looking for people with guns; we're looking for car parts. We got a tip there's a chop shop operating in Arlington, so you watch that truck of yours."

"Will do." With his mission accomplished, Gabe got up to leave. "Thanks for the warning."

"Anytime," Willis said, coming around the desk to clap him on the back and walk him to the door. "Consider it a professional courtesy. You watch your back."

"Always do." Another old habit that died hard.

Once outside in the cold, Gabe climbed into his truck, gathering his coat and his thoughts around him. No news would have been good news, and any news was bad news. This was bad. He hadn't expected Bookman to be on the loose.

At least the marshals hadn't focused any serious attention on Washington as an escape route for their star witness. Willis would have spilled that too. He didn't, so Emma must have done a decent job of covering her tracks.

Didn't matter though, she was an amateur. A decent job wasn't perfect. If they wanted her bad enough, they would eventually find her.

Gabe started the truck and let it idle for a minute as he reminded himself that in this case the good guys and the bad guys were on the same team. If the good guys didn't know where Emma had run yet, then maybe the bad guys didn't either. He frowned as he realized what a self-serving piece of logic he'd concocted to make himself feel better.

Only a wet-behind-the-ears ensign would buy that, Gabriel. And to make matters worse, you've got that feeling again, like somebody's breathing down your neck.

He knew better than to ignore the sixth sense that sent him to the police department in the first place. Gabe was playing a deadly game of chicken with very little to go on. How long was too long to wait to hear from Patrick before he moved Emma? He wrestled with that question the rest of the dày, because somewhere out there, the opponent was on the move.

And maybe there were two of them now.

SEVEN

Emily stared out the window of Marsha Jean's double wide trailer at the split rail fence that framed a tiny yard. In one corner two bicycles leaned against the rails. Snow drifted almost to the wheel hubs and piled high on the seats like an extra-thick layer of padding or an avalanche waiting to happen. The well-used sled leaning next to the gate should have made her smile, should have made her remember the carefree childhood joy of racing down a hill.

But she couldn't call up those memories. All she could remember was one particularly joyless ride. A tree had somehow jumped into her path. She remembered the breathless excitement vanishing suddenly. In its place came a split second of agonizingly real terror. But that second seemed to go on forever before she finally crashed.

Those long-ago emotions were so clear, because that's how she felt now. Emily hugged herself and tried to shake the nagging fear that colored everything she saw. But she couldn't do that either.

Beyond the fence was rugged country, hills and trees dusted with white, a road that scarcely deserved the name. It should have been a beautiful scene of peace, but not to Emily. To her the landscape felt unnaturally quiet, almost threatening, because she couldn't forget that a savage reality hid behind the serene beauty.

Gabe's protection was like the landscape. Reality hid behind the pretend safety, waiting for her to let down her guard, waiting for her to make a mistake. Mistakes would be so easy to make right now; she was tired. Since Idaho she'd jumped at every sound, every silence, every shadow, every heartbeat. Every night.

Surrounded by the warm chaos of Marsha Jean's home, the contrast between her life and the waitress's became a hot knife that sliced and burned its way through the lies she fed herself, peeling away the last of her illusions. She was never going to have peace. Her future wouldn't be any more "normal" than her past.

For twenty years ice skating had run her life. Now survival was going to take over the job of taskmaster, forcing her to run and keep running. Forcing her to move when anyone got too close. Emily actually envied the waitress her trailer, her two kids, and the pile of dirty dishes in the sink. At least it was normal. At least it was a home.

"My Eddie used to stand there for hours," Marsha Jean said, breaking into her thoughts.

Emily pulled herself away from the view. "It's gorgeous."

"That's why we bought the place. Eddie got sick

before we could build a house. And when he was gone—" For the first time since she'd met her, Marsha Jean lost some of her brassy confidence. She shrugged. "I didn't have the heart to build our house. It wouldn't have seemed right. Now it's just me and the two kids, but that view keeps me going. We don't have anything like that down south. Not even close!"

The snap was back in her voice on that last sentence, obviously she didn't let much keep her down. Emily asked the obvious question, "What is it that you *do* have in the South?"

"Deer season."

Emily laughed and came away from the window. "Deer season?"

"Oh, yeah. Deer season and pick-'em-up trucks with gun racks. The two coming-of-age rituals—cruising for girls and gunning for deer."

"Oh, come on. It's not that bad."

"Oh, but it is. Our menfolk pride themselves on a Zenlike dedication to putting deer meat in the freezer and on the table." Marsha Jean picked up a pair of orange-handled scissors. "We have getting ready for deer season, bow season, doe season, regular season, rehashing the season, and talking about next season."

"Then I guess they must be pretty good at it."

Waggling her finger, Marsha Jean said, "I believe they could get a lesson or two from you. I don't think any of them can bag a buck as fast as you. My hat's off. You managed to make old Gabe fall in love, and I had given up on him. The man's a hard case. Hopeless. Or was."

Emily choked back a laugh. She hadn't "bagged"

anyone, certainly not Gabe. "Why'd you think Gabe was hopeless?"

"That man can freeze a woman cold in her tracks with one of those get-out-of-my-life stares of his, and he hasn't had a date since he came to town, *despite* my best efforts to fix him up. Of course, I didn't know he was savin' himself for you." Marsha Jean smiled mischievously. "Judging from what I saw this morning, it was worth savin' up."

Startled, Emily realized that's exactly what kissing Gabe felt like—like she'd been saving up all her life. Then she realized that she didn't want to feel that way about any man, not now. Especially not Gabe. She didn't want any kind of bond with him beyond gratitude. She didn't want to become attached to anyone and have circumstances rip them away from her. Only fools expected happy endings.

"Can't put it off any longer, girlfriend." Marsha Jean pulled out a dining room chair and made snipping motions in the air with her scissors. "While I whack off that gorgeous head of hair, you can tell me how you and Gabe met. This story has to be good. Did he save you from terrorists or something?"

"Or something," Emily said softly as she sat down, but before she could tell sweet Marsha Jean a pack of lies, the fear inside turned to terror.

The unmistakable crack of a rifle forced a scream from her throat.

Gabe cleaned up the broken glass and spent the rest of the afternoon surfing a computer information network. He learned a few things about Emily Quinn that made him feel better about her chances. If ice skating had had such a thing as a photo finish, then that was how close she'd come to two Olympic golds. Always a bridesmaid, never a bride.

She never quit though; she just kept trying. Even after the accident and her parents' death, she went back to the rink. Only that time the fairy tale ended for good. No amount of grit or determination could change the nerve damage to her ankle.

When he finished on the computer, Gabe shut it down, hoping the woman still had some of that grit. She was going to need it. Shaking off a feeling of uneasiness, Gabe resisted the urge to call Marsha Jean and check on their progress. They knew the plan. They'd call if there was a problem. Despite Marsha Jean's flip attitude, she was trustworthy.

Instead of dialing, he made himself check the weather report and inventory his booze supply. This time of year the roads were as liable to close as not. He couldn't afford to be cut off from his supplier with less than a full stockroom when the storm hit the following night. Quiet crowds turned ugly when a bar ran out of liquor.

However, booze would be the least of his worries if the storm got bad enough to close the roads. The real problem would be getting Emma out of town. That morning's chat with Willis had changed his plans. Originally Gabe intended to stall Emma until he heard from Patrick. Not anymore.

If he didn't hear soon, all bets were off. The clock was ticking, he could feel it. That troublesome sixth sense was bothering him, poking him, tapping him on the shoulder, and telling him to get the hell out of Dodge.

Three days, Gabe promised himself, and then Emma disappeared.

Besides, he thought with gallows humor, three days would be plenty of time for Emma to finish cleaning his entire apartment. The woman lived to clean. When he'd come out of the shower that morning, the sparkling kitchen appliances had almost blinded him. He caught himself smiling at the memory as he hauled a case of beer from the back to reload the cooler before the first customers straggled in.

He didn't need or want a maid, but cleaning his house seemed to give Emma some sense of having evened the score, a sense that she was paying him back for the roof over her head. In her place he'd have done the same thing. He hated charity. Didn't mind giving it, just hated taking it. Hated debts. She appeared to share the same opinion.

Accordingly, he and Emma had worked out a system. She pretended his place was a pigsty desperately in need of cleaning before the health department condemned it, and he pretended that he didn't care whether or not it ever got clean. She didn't have to say thank you, and he didn't have to say you're welcome.

Which was good. Because they'd barely exchanged two dozen words once he'd gotten out of the shower. Emma stared at his clean-shaven jaw for a long time, got pink across her cheeks, and muttered something about getting dressed to go with Marsha Jean.

The next thing he knew she was in that shapeless

gray sack she called a habit—sans veil. But it wasn't the habit that irritated him. It was the red silk panties and matching bra he knew she wore beneath the habit. The thought of her underwear was enough to make him reconsider his plan to change her looks. *Emily Quinn* couldn't leave the apartment.

Yep, keeping her confined and wearing red silk undies with only him for company had definite possibilities. All of them foolish.

So he had shooed her out the door with Marsha Jean. That was hours before. By now it was too late to change his mind about anything. The deed was already done. Customers were drifting into the bar.

Sunday nights were usually slow but profitable for Gabe. He opened at six P.M. and closed at eleven. Served more brain grenades—beer—than anything else. The crowd was never more than a dozen or so people at any one time, and quiet for the most part. Tonight was no exception; he could handle the bar business and Emma too. Especially since Clayton Dover and Sawyer Johns hadn't worked up the courage to show their faces around the bar yet.

A couple of strangers mixed in with the familiar faces. That wasn't unusual either, but tonight every stranger was a threat to Emma's safety. These strangers were drinking hard liquor and asking no questions. A good sign. They behaved like ordinary men trying to drown their sorrow in private, but he watched them all the same.

Beneath their heavy winter coats they wore loose jackets, loose enough to easily conceal a weapon. Since Gabe couldn't pat them down without arousing suspicion, he made it his personal mission to know when and how deeply they breathed.

A half hour later Gabe checked the clock for the third time. He didn't like it. His waitress was overdue to make an appearance. And so was his sweet little "cousin" from Indiana, who'd come all this way for the big family reunion.

No sooner had he reached for the phone than Marsha Jean came sauntering in with a big grin and a sad story about car trouble. "Oh, Gabe! I am so sorry, but that vicious car battery of mine decided to poop out just as I was leaving the house! I had to call a neighbor to give me a jump."

"I told you last week to get a new battery," he said as calmly as he could.

"And I told you to give me a raise." She winked at him as she tossed her purse under the counter and shrugged out of her coat. Tonight's T-shirt announced STUPID PEOPLE SHOULDN'T BREED.

"How are the kids?" Gabe asked, but meant something entirely different. "I'm going to have to make a point to see them."

"Soon." Marsha Jean understood him perfectly. She grabbed a bar towel and tucked it in her jeans. "They're changing so much, you wouldn't recognize them from day to day!"

"Good."

"Sometimes I don't recognize them myself. Like today, when we heard a rifle shot." She paused, gauging his response to that little tidbit before she continued. "It turned out to be some hunter, but it scared the little girl to death. Heck, her scream almost scared me to death."

Shooting a glance quickly around the bar, Gabe lowered his voice. "She okay?"

"Oh, yeah. She's fine. Now. A little vague on why she reacted that way." He could tell that his waitress wasn't a bit happy about being kept in the dark, but a customer wandered up to the bar. Marsha Jean reverted to code. "You know how a mother worries. I was hoping you would tell me something to make me feel better."

"I doubt it."

"That's what I was afraid of. Then it's tit for tat." The blonde sighed and turned to the three guys now sitting at the bar. "Lord! It's like a morgue in here," she pronounced with enthusiasm. "We need some music! Let me just go fix that. I think something with a nice, slow beat is what we need. And, Gabe, I think Angus needs a refill."

Absently Gabe handed a Mexican beer to Angus Deady, who catered to the tourist trade by running raft trips down the Wenatchee and Klickitat rivers. The early nasty winter had pretty much shut him down, and he liked to drown his sorrows in foreign beer. But Gabe's mind wasn't on his customers and their troubles. It was on the two strangers and the dangerous payback gleam he saw in Marsha Jean's eyes.

She was mighty pleased about something all of a sudden, and he assumed she was keeping a secret of her own. For the next fifteen minutes she avoided him, making sure to put her orders in and pick them up while standing next to Angus. That way Gabe couldn't ask her any questions, and she could snicker to her heart's content.

Just as he considered dragging her into the stockroom to demand an explanation for that damned grin, the new and improved Emily Quinn walked through the front door. Even before she let the worn-out green parka slide off her shoulders, he knew this incarnation was a far cry from the nun. There were some similarities, like the holier-than-thou blue jeans, but overall the woman looked like she'd fallen from grace a long time before and real hard.

"Gabe!" she said, loud enough to get everyone's attention, and set down a small battered suitcase. Whispered conversations around the bar stopped as his customers swiveled to get an eyeful.

That was part of the plan, but the hello-throw-me-down red sweater and the appreciative whistles from the crowd were not. Neither was his reaction. Every muscle in his body went on alert, and he was ready to pound every man who so much as noticed Emma's obvious attributes. Of course, those attributes were hard to miss in that sweater.

Oblivious of it all, Emma shook out the new, sexy, and shaggy mop of streaked honey-blond hair that came just below her shoulders. Gabe realized that if he didn't do something soon, he'd have to beat the guys off her with Jeffie's baseball bat. He threw a bone to his pride by silently insisting that his concern for Emma was only natural given his role in this mess. He was supposed to be protecting her, keeping her out of the limelight. With the drooling idiots falling all over themselves to get a date, how long would it be before one of them recognized her and ruined everything?

He glanced at Marsha Jean, who batted her eyelashes and looked as innocent as a newborn babe. As he passed her, he paused long enough to say under his breath, "I wanted *average*, dammit. Average looks, average hair, average clothes."

"Then maybe you should have given me average to work with," Marsha Jean whispered back, laughing.

"Emma!" Gabe forced out as cheerfully as he could. They'd decided that for the time being Emma would be the least confusing name for her to answer to, and for him to remember.

He didn't even realize he was scowling until she backed up and said, "Whoa, Gabe! I know it's been a long time, but aren't you the least little bit glad to see me?"

One of the guys in the crowd yelled, "If he's not, I sure as hell am, baby doll!"

Even Angus cheered up long enough to agree with that sentiment, pounding his bottle on the bar. "I'll buy you a beer to prove it! Barkeep! A beer for the lady!"

A second later Emma had her pick of drink offers. But Angus's offer to take her for a river ride she wouldn't forget was the last straw. Gabe decided there was only one way to put a stop to this infantile innuendo and macho posturing. So he walked right up to her, grabbed her around the waist, and kissed her in front of God and everybody.

Emily's world tilted and all of her carefully rehearsed lines went sliding off into oblivion. She'd expected an awkward family-reunion-style peck on the cheek, but not this. As always, the first touch of his lips and breach of his tongue brought the flutter of panic, excitement, and pleasure that started deep in her belly. Her arms went around his neck of their own volition, and then she felt herself lifted up as Gabe caught her to his chest. Almost before he'd begun, he stopped, but the stunned silence around them was witness to the fact that this had been no ordinary kiss.

The wolf whistles and catcalls started as he set her on her feet.

"All right, Gabe!"

"The iceman cracketh!"

The last comment jolted Emily back to reality. This intense kiss in the middle of a crowded room was totally out of character for the man who never revealed himself or lost control. Amid the commotion she whispered, "What was *that* all about?"

"Change of plans," he told her as he bent over to retrieve her parka from the floor. Somehow during the kiss, Emily had lost her grip on it as well as reality.

"Thanks for the warning! What are we supposed to be now?" she inquired politely as he handed it to her. "Kissing cousins?"

"A shame Marsha Jean didn't make over your mouth," he observed congenially, and turned to the crowd. Gabe dropped an arm protectively over her shoulders. "All you boys can put your water pistols back in your pockets. This is Emma Gabriel, my ex-wife. As you can see, we've had some trouble getting used to the 'ex' part."

"Actually, it was the marriage part that we had trouble getting used to," Emily volunteered, getting into the spirit of the moment. Gabe was not impressed with her help.

He picked up her suitcase and circled her waist, cinching her close, possessively. If he'd had the words "property of Christian Gabriel" tattooed across her forehead, his message couldn't have been clearer. For the slow learners, he added, "Maybe if we keep practicing we'll figure out how to do this relationship thing right. Now, if you'll excuse us, I'll get her settled in. *Upstairs*. Marsha Jean! You've got some dry customers over here."

The way he hauled her around through the crowd toward the stairwell door, Emily decided he had more than enough upper-body strength to have been a pairs skater. However, he rated a big fat zero in the grace department. For the sake of the plan she smiled and simpered and generally let him have his Neanderthal moment until the EMPLOYEES ONLY door closed behind them.

When they were alone in the dark, she elbowed him as hard as she could and was rewarded with an "Uff." Turning on him, she kept her voice down but the anger was obvious nonetheless. "What the hell do you think you are doing, telling everyone that I'm Emma *Gabriel*?"

"I'm doing you a favor. Being my ex-wife will keep the boys from getting any ideas about getting cozy." He set the suitcase down on the first stair.

She gaped at him and pulled her sweater down to cover the waistband of her jeans. "What business is it of yours who I get cozy with *anyway*? It's not like I'm really your ex-wife! And that's another problem! How many ex–Mrs. Gabriels are there? Seeing as how I've been *married* to you, I should at least know which number wife I am."

"You're it."

"Really?" she asked, startled. Somehow she had expected Gabe to have a real ex-wife or wives. Like Patrick, who had spoken fondly and with regret about his two failed marriages, both shipwrecked by the demands of his navy career and the long separations.

"Really," he repeated. "You're it. So calm down. This little alteration in the plan was necessary because you and Marsha Jean got carried away. Tonight's experiment was to see if we could pass you off in a safe setting. Now, how long do you think it would take before one of those lumberjacks recognized you while he was hanging all over you, looking into those damned green eyes, listening to you talk, trying to get a date?"

Emily backed up a step, surprised that he knew her eyes were green. The stairwell was too dark for him to see the color, which meant he'd noticed and remembered. Before she let herself get too warm and fuzzy, she reminded herself that Gabe was trained to be observant.

Back on the attack, she said, "Gabe, you were the one who said to forget the glasses."

"That's because it's obvious they don't belong to you. They're too big for your face, and you squint in them. You're supposed to look normal. The whole point of this charade was for you *not* to call attention to yourself."

"And I thought the whole point of this little charade of ours was for me to interact with people and see if your customers would recognize me! Well, so far—in the five seconds you gave them to look at me—they haven't!"

He didn't argue, but disapproval leaked from every pore in his body, filling the air around her.

"Okay, Gabe. Out with it. You've got something you want to say, so just say it, and we can get back to the bar before Marsha Jean sends a search party."

Silence reigned as Gabe struggled with a response. "I don't like it."

"Don't like what?" she asked instantly, assuming the worst. "Is someone out there?"

"No."

In a rush she let out the breath she'd been holding. "Then what?"

"I don't like it. That's all. I don't like the way you look. I don't like the way they look at you."

Exasperation began to get the best of her, and she had to struggle to keep her voice low so she couldn't be heard in the bar. The customers thought they were up-stairs putting away her things or— Emily didn't want to contemplate what people thought she and Gabe were doing.

Dragging herself back to the conversation, she re-minded him, "This whole game was *your* idea. If you will recall, I was happy with the nun's habit!"

"You were supposed to be my *mousy* little cousin from Indiana."

"Right. Old clothes, tacky makeup, and a bad hair-cut. We did our part. I don't look like me. Not at first glance. I've never worn a pair of blue jeans with a hole in them in my life. When I can afford colored contact lenses, it'll be even better."

"You look like you were poured into those jeans."

"That's because I was! I had to lie down on the bed to zip the damned things up. They must be a boy's cut 'cause all of me doesn't fit in here the way it's supposed to."

Gabe didn't need to have that particular fact pointed out. "Surely you could at least have found a sweater the right size!"

Emily snorted. "Look, Gabe. I didn't pick out these clothes. You're the one who told Marsha Jean how small I was, while I sat right in your living room telling her that I was bigger than I looked. *If you get my drift.* But neither of you bothered to listen to me. I guess you thought I was being falsely modest. Or maybe you thought *you* knew best because you'd handled the merchandise! So now we're both stuck with these clothes."

Grabbing the doorknob, Emma gave him one last point to ponder before she pulled it open. "Have you taken a look at the size of your hands lately? They'd make almost anything look small. I think you need a new yardstick, buddy. And I need a drink. I've had one helluva day."

With that parting shot, she walked back into the smoky bar and left Gabe wondering if he'd created a monster. He followed her out, trying to ignore the sway in her nicely rounded hips. Unfortunately, Gabe felt compelled to single out a few of his patrons for stern looks when their eyes strayed to Emma's chest for too long.

Since the previous night's fight had obviously made the town's gossip hotline, none of them seemed willing to risk his displeasure or a confrontation. The offending parties became suddenly engrossed in the labels of their beer bottles or in lighting cigarettes. A couple of them even had the good sense to get up and move in the other direction.

Their willingness to honor his claim to Emma should have erased the vague discontent in his gut, but it didn't. They weren't responsible for his unease, Gabe realized. Emma was.

Having to play the role of her possessive ex-husband, having to pass her off as his, only made him more aware that he had no real claim to Emma. No right to protect her beyond his job as a bodyguard. His whole posture was a sham. She wasn't his. And wanting what he couldn't have was foolish. He'd learned that lesson all too well.

Marsha Jean was waiting for them beside the bar, and she was loaded for bear. Gabe doubted she believed the love-affair story anymore. "It is so nice to meet you, Mrs. Gabriel! Gabe"—she threw a sour look in his direction—"hasn't told me one blessed thing about you. So you'll have to fill in all the blanks!"

"Call me, Emma," Emily suggested as she hopped up on a stool, forgetting how tight the jeans were. She sucked in a breath as they threatened to cut off the circulation at the bend of her thigh and hip, and at her waist.

"I'm Marsha Jean Petit." The blond waitress stuck her hand out just as if they'd never met before. "Can he get you a drink?"

"Yeah. A Virgin Mary would be nice." Emily adjusted her position until the pressure eased up. "I don't think I can afford the calories in anything alcoholic."

"Why is it that all the good stuff is bad for us, or causes us so much trouble in the long run?" Marsha

Jean asked that question, looking straight at Gabe. "Take men, for example—"

"Marsha Jean," Gabe warned as his waitress started to climb up on a stool beside Emma. "You have customers."

"Oh, don't worry," she said, and settled onto the stool. "I just gave everybody another round on the house in celebration of Mrs. Gabriel's return." Leaning until her shoulder touched Angus's shoulder, she asked, "You don't mind if I sit here and talk to Emma?"

"No, ma'am. I actually couldn't be any happier unless you sat on my lap."

"See there, Gabe," Emily said. "The customers are happy. Could I have that drink?"

"I don't know," he answered. "Can you pay for it?"

"I will," Angus and one of the strangers volunteered in unison.

Without saying a word, Gabe turned and focused his attention on the stranger first. He was a pale guy, easy to dismiss as all talk and no action—except for the coolness in his eyes. He didn't flinch, but he did pick up his drink.

Looking at Emma, he said, "Sorry, ma'am. Maybe the next round." Then he found an empty table.

Next Gabe considered Angus. He didn't frown. He didn't raise an eyebrow. He didn't glare.

Nevertheless, Angus blanched and stammered, "Sorry, Gabe. I don't know what came over me."

"Generosity," Emily declared as she pivoted toward Gabe and tapped him on the knuckles. "It was a random act of kindness. You do know what that is, don't you?"

"Yeah." Gabe nodded, his gaze locked with hers.

"It's like when someone takes in a stray, and feeds it, and cares for it, and keeps it safe from the big bad world."

"And has it neutered, most likely," Emily added under her breath.

"It depends," Gabe said.

"On what?" Marsha Jean asked, entirely missing the undercurrent that surged between her boss and Emily.

"On whether the stray bites the hand that feeds it."

"Suppose it was just one tiny nip," Emily whispered, caught up in the heat of his gaze.

"One?"

"Uh-huh. Just one . . . soft . . . nip." Emily put the side of her index finger in her mouth and gently dragged her teeth along the skin to the tip.

"I've always believed that one good nip deserves another."

"Oh, my," Marsha Jean said as she realized they weren't talking about strays any longer. "Angus darlin', dance with me! I feel a hormonal rampage comin' on. I need an outlet."

Happy to oblige, Angus did as he was told.

As they left, Emily wanted to call them back, tell them not to leave her. Without them she felt exposed. Any fool knew there was safety in numbers.

"How 'bout that drink?" Gabe asked.

"I can't pay for it."

"We'll think of something," he promised. "Maybe you could help me behind the bar."

"Doing what?" she asked suspiciously.

"Whatever needs doing." He grinned. "Like cutting

limes and lemons. Like running the cash register. Nothing hard back here at all."

"I'll bet." But Emily got up anyway. She didn't mind working for her supper or her drinks. In the process of getting off the stool, she thrust her chest out, unaware of the effect the simple movement had on Gabe.

Once she had joined him behind the bar, it was all Gabe could do not to inspect his hands to see if they were as big as Emma seemed to think. He realized they were when she was trying to learn the cash register and he reached over to show her how to unjam the keys, which resembled manual typewriter keys. Their hands rested side by side for a moment, the edge of their palms touching. Fascinated by the difference, Gabe forgot what he'd been about to show her. Months of experience at operating the cantankerous old cash register evaporated from his brain.

"See. I told you they were big," Emma told him with great satisfaction.

She surprised him then. She looked up into his face and smiled. No, she grinned. The first one of those he'd seen, and he knew he was fighting a losing battle. He was going to get attached to Emily Quinn, and he wasn't going to be able to do a damn thing about it. Except watch her walk away when she didn't need him anymore.

The rest of the evening was like watching a flower unfold as Emma became more confident in her new persona, though she never strayed far from him. He kept one eye on Emma, and one on the pale stranger. But mostly an eye on Emma.

"Emma," Marsha Jean begged as she grabbed another round of beers for the back booth, "I got my hands full tonight, and the guy over there in the black sweater just signaled for another beer. Take it for me?"

"No problem." Emily looked up just as the man Marsha Jean indicated was turning away. A feeling of déjà vu swamped her, made her dizzy for a moment, nauseated. Her mind registered his dark hair and the tilt of his head.

Suddenly she was right back in the farmhouse, facing the man with the gun.

EIGHT

When Emma's hand sagged away from taking the bottle, Gabe steadied her, simultaneously scanning the bar. He checked the pale man, but he was absorbed in his drink. The other stranger had cleared out an hour earlier.

Knowing he'd missed something, Gabe let his gaze track Marsha Jean as she passed through the crowd with a heavy tray of drinks. And that's when he saw him, an unfamiliar guy in a black sweater. Gabe's mind raced, trying to assess the damage even though the man ignored them.

Dammit! Who the hell was he and where had he come from? More important, how long had he been there?

Those were questions Gabe shouldn't have had to ask, and he knew it. He was a fool. He got sidetracked by the obvious and wrapped up in his proprietary feelings for Emma. If he didn't stay sharp, he'd get them both killed.

Gabe walked her back a few steps, putting himself

between her and the rest of the room. He let his free hand stray toward the shelf beneath the register. "Tell me what happened."

"For a second, I thought . . ." Her voice faded uncertainly as she continued to stare around his body.

As his fingers inched beneath the towels covering his gun, he asked, "Thought what?"

"He—" She looked up into his eyes, her fear evident, her voice uncertain. "For a second, something about that customer, the one Marsha Jean wanted me to take the beer to . . . something about the way he turned made me think of what happened, made me think it was *him*. But now I don't know. I'm not sure anymore."

"Thought it was who? The gunman in the farmhouse?" Gabe asked quietly, and risked another glance at the man.

She nodded. "I just went cold inside when I saw him. And then . . . nothing." Words tumbled out of her as she tried to explain her instincts away. "The feeling faded, and now I'm wondering if I imagined the whole thing. Maybe I'm just edgy. Maybe I'm looking for a monster behind every bush because of that rifle shot at Marsha Jean's."

"Take a deep breath and calm down." When she did, he asked, "Did you get a good look at the man who shot the deputy marshal?"

"No. Not full on," she whispered. "That night when he turned around I was so scared that I couldn't see anything but the gun, and then I closed my eyes. The next thing I knew he was on the floor. I didn't look when I walked by him. I couldn't. I was trying to get to—to the marshal that was shot."

"Hey, you two lovebirds! We got customers, you know," Marsha Jean reminded them as she slapped her tray on the bar. "So let's hop to it!"

"Been waiting on you, darlin'," Gabe said, forcing himself to sound at ease. He managed to turn around while still shielding Emma and slid the beer toward the end of the bar in a smooth, fluid motion. "Take that to the gentleman with the black sweater. Then check the booth in the back. They haven't ordered in a while."

Marsha Jean eyed them thoughtfully. "You trying to get rid of me, boss?"

"How perceptive of you." He increased the pressure on Emma's arm, warning her to be quiet. "Now go away."

Marsha Jean took the beer, but she warned him, "I love secrets. I'll figure it out. Just you wait."

As she left, Emily shook her head anxiously. "I don't like this, Gabe. Marsha Jean suspects something already, and you're sending her over there?"

"Shh . . . it's all right. I think I know what happened—why you thought you knew him and now you're not sure. Look at him," Gabe ordered her. "Who does he remind you of?"

Emily stared for a minute as the man took the beer from Marsha Jean and cocked his head back, laughing at something she said. He obviously gave as good as he got, because Marsha Jean appeared flustered for a moment. Then she smiled, a calculating smile as if the man's credit with her had unexpectedly gone up a notch.

"He reminds me of Patrick," she said slowly. "Same color hair, same body type, same profile."

"And that's why you freaked. You've been running on emotional empty for four days, expecting the bad guy to catch you. You saw something familiar, your mind confused the signals, and you scared the hell out of yourself."

"That sounds so simple," Emily said, wanting to believe him, but her memory nagged her, reminding her that she had mistaken the gunman for Patrick once already.

But that was the silver gun, and the suit. Wasn't it? She couldn't be sure. And she couldn't explain it to Gabe without telling him about Patrick.

"Believe me. It's simple. The only woman he wants tonight is Marsha Jean," Gabe told her, but silently he revised his own timetable, shaving off a day. Better safe than sorry.

Tomorrow was Monday. He'd give Patrick until Tuesday morning. If he didn't call by then, it wouldn't matter. He and Emma would be gone.

Gabe was going with her. At least until she was safe. A woman who froze the way she did wasn't ready to take on the task of protecting herself. If they caught up with her, she'd be dead before she decided what to do.

"But what if next time it *is* someone after me?" she asked him quietly. "Maybe I should go. I can't stand the thought that Marsha Jean or anyone else would be in danger because of me. I don't want anything to happen to her. Or you. Not because of me."

"Nothing's going to happen. I'm not going to let it," Gabe told her firmly, and turned her toward the

EMPLOYEES ONLY door. He leaned close to her ear. "Why don't you call it a night and go upstairs," he suggested. "It's almost closing time."

Emily tried not to let the way Gabe rubbed her shoulders affect her, but it did. He had a way of melting the tension in her muscles and replacing it with heat that was just as devastating to her nerves. Right now he tempted her with the promise that he'd take care of her. The promise was as seductive as his touch. Her heart was only now returning to normal rhythm, and he'd set it off again.

When she hesitated, he added, "I've got to stay downstairs and clean up. You'd just be in the way. Go. Feed Wart. Take a shower. Relax." He tried to massage her shoulders, but she pulled away as if burned.

"All right," she agreed, and took a deep breath. He wondered if the breath was meant to help her get across the room without running, or because he'd touched her.

Gabe watched as she said a quick good-night to Marsha Jean. Then he eyed the man in the black sweater, making certain that his gaze didn't linger on Emma. It didn't. Nevertheless Gabe continued to watch him.

The man left shortly before last call. He was agile on his feet; he had a balance that hinted at training of some sort. That didn't mean he was after Emma, Gabe reminded himself. Emma's fright had started his imagination working overtime, but he'd rather be prepared. He couldn't afford another mistake. The men after Emma didn't take prisoners, they played for keeps.

When everyone was gone, Marsha Jean put on her coat and started to say good-bye. Instead, she snapped her fingers and told him to hold off locking up while she ran out to her car. She came back in with a pair of figure skates.

"I keep these in my trunk along with Annabelle's. Since Emily and I wear the same size shoe, I thought I'd leave them here."

"What for?"

"She might like a chance to glide around Sutter's Pond without reporters and coaches watching."

Gabe wasn't certain she was serious. "Have you lost your mind?"

"Hey, it's only a couple of miles away, so close she could walk. It's completely deserted during the week. You know that. And so does she. I told her."

"Doesn't matter. She's not going skating. She's not going anywhere without me. And I'm not going skating."

"Well, the skates are here just in case." Marsha Jean put them on the bar, but she looked like a woman who had something more to say. After a brief pause she spit it out. "You aren't having an affair, are you? She's in trouble. I mean real trouble."

Gabe didn't see the sense in lying. He nodded.

"You be careful with her, then. From what I saw today, I'd imagine bein' in her skin is a little like bein' in a pressure cooker with no release valve. Skating might help."

"It's too risky."

She didn't argue. She just shrugged and headed for the door. "You be careful with *you* too. I've gotten kind of used to having you around."

"I'm always careful." *Except tonight*, his conscience added.

Gabe locked the door behind her, checked it twice, and began to clean up. He took his time polishing the bar. He wasn't certain he could sit and listen to Emma take a shower without losing his mind.

They might not be having an affair, but he'd gotten all tangled up in the woman somehow. She had him thinking stupid, and that was a dangerous way to think.

Never in his life had he felt so possessive of a woman, as if it were his job to protect her from everything in the world that might hurt her. Patrick wasn't the only SEAL with a thing for scared strays.

Takes one to know one. That's what he'd been all his life—a stray that no one adopted.

He stared at his big hands and admitted the spitfire who'd come out of Marsha Jean's Clairol bottle would be a handful, even for him. Tonight for the first time he'd seen the energy that had taken her to so many world titles. That energy was as seductive as her softness had been. And then right before she went upstairs, a little of the old Emma—the uncertain one, the shy one—crept back into the new Emma.

They were going to have to come to an understanding about the chemistry between them. Otherwise they'd be walking on eggshells, and Gabe didn't want to walk on eggshells.

Uncertain which Emma waited for him in his apartment, he climbed the stairs. When he looked at the place, he realized she'd been cleaning again. No question about that. The coffee table actually resembled a coffee table instead of a lost and found department.

Wart meowed a lazy greeting, and Emma stepped out of the kitchen. The movement caught his eye and his sense of the absurd. Gabe laughed outright, the tension inside him snapping.

"Pajamas with feet?" he queried when his spontaneous outburst subsided.

"I was lucky Marsha Jean found any at all," she informed him primly, and smoothed the blue and white checked flannel. "They happen to be quite trendy and practical."

"Yeah," he agreed. "If you're four years old and keep losing your slippers. Or if you're trying to run off the man in your life."

Gabe's amusement died as Emma averted her gaze, and he realized that he'd stumbled on the truth with his wisecrack. Emma's pajamas were a no-trespassing sign. He got the message loud and clear. The charming Emma Gabriel, ex-wife with the ready smile, was nothing more than a character in a play.

After all, she was used to performing. Wasn't that what figure skating was? A performance sport?

Wise up, Gabe. The woman cozied up and hung around you tonight because she was scared and you were handy.

But even given her desperate circumstances, the classy Emily Quinn wouldn't waste her time on a flat-broke, ex–Navy SEAL with no prospects beyond bartending. He was useful and nothing more. *Silk and flannel*, he reminded himself. *Cut from a different cloth.*

Even when she was the one in flannel.

Carefully controlling his voice, he asked, "Did Marsha Jean find anything *normal* in the rummage bin?"

As a matter of fact she had, but Emily wasn't volunteering that information. She didn't intend to wear the satin nightshirt because it was cut down to her belly button. Afraid he'd know she was lying if she didn't meet his eyes, she lifted her chin to answer, and was caught off guard by the anger smoldering in Gabe's dark gaze.

Nothing in his voice had prepared her for the way he looked at her. This was the intense man who had sized her up and dismissed her that first night in the bar. Gabe was the kind of man who could be angry at the world and never waste a breath on complaint. He kept so much inside, and right now he was unhappy with her.

She didn't even know why. She didn't like it though. Ironically, she wanted to make it better, but she had no idea where to start. Gabe wouldn't help her. Helping her would be against the code—the code of the strong, silent type. Gabe was a hard man with hard rules, and she'd obviously broken one of them without even knowing it.

He probably learned this little technique for controlling people in officer candidate school. Keep the troops guessing. Keep them thinking they've done something wrong and they'd fall all over themselves trying to fix it. She figured her coaches had attended the same classes.

"Look, Gabe, I'm too tired to debate sleepwear fashions." *Or to play mind games with you.* "Can't we just arm-wrestle for the bed and get some sleep?"

"We both know that wouldn't be a fair contest."

"That's the point." She padded over to the bed, got her pillow from last night, and lifted the blanket off the end. "It's your house, so you get the bed. I'm the guest, so I sleep on the couch."

He didn't move away from the couch, so she tried again. "Gabe, I appreciate your wanting to be kind or chivalrous or whatever. I do. But common sense alone will tell you that I actually fit on the couch comfortably. You don't."

"All right." He knew better than to argue with a woman who had her mind made up. "Whatever you want."

By the time Gabe had showered and changed into some jogging pants and a T-shirt, Emma had her nose buried in the pillow and her eyes squeezed shut, pretending to be asleep. Before he switched off the lights, he turned the stereo down low and put in a CD of old blues tunes. The sad music fit his melancholy mood. The world was damned unfair. Always dangling what he couldn't have right in front of his nose.

A harmonica wailed softly about injustice as he killed the last light.

"'Night, Gabe," Emma said softly when the bed creaked under his weight.

Surprised by the faint words, Gabe didn't answer right away. He rolled over on his back and put his hands behind his head, staring at the ceiling. Her whisper was the same clandestine sound he'd heard for so many years at the orphanage—the kind of whisper people used in the dark when they were afraid of being caught or of waking someone.

Who was she afraid of waking?

And then Gabe realized, she was afraid of him. She didn't want to wake him—arouse him. She was scared of him. Of the fact that he could make her respond on a sensual level.

A long time later, he said, "'Night, Emma."

"My name is Emily," she corrected him in the same quiet, hesitant voice. "Even when we're alone you don't call me that."

"Do you want me to?"

"No." It was her turn for silence, and then another question. "I just wondered why? Are you afraid you'll slip?"

Gabe was tired of walking on eggshells. So he told her. "Emily belongs to them. Emma is mine."

Closing her eyes, Emily fought the intimacy of his words, fought the seduction of the dark. *Emma is mine.* Those three words had such incredible power. This declaration had nothing to do with the way he'd laid claim to her in the bar. This was about wanting the imperfect woman beneath the ice princess. No one had ever wanted that woman before. No one had ever known she was there.

With three words he'd managed to knock down most of the wall she'd built between them. The wall was supposed to keep her from doing something foolish, like completely trusting anyone. But the darkness encouraged confidences, and she was afraid to go to sleep. So she kept talking, pretending that they were having an innocent conversation.

"My granddad had a nickname for me. He used to call me Emmy Sue."

"Was he a skater?"

"Good Lord, no. He didn't know a thing about ice skating, but he built the most beautiful birdhouses for me. Most of the time I couldn't tell one bird from another, but I loved to watch them land and take off. They were so graceful."

"So were you."

"Excuse me?"

"I am always amazed at what a person with a computer can find out if he knows his way around the Internet system."

"You researched me?" She wasn't sure whether to be offended or flattered.

"For instance, I found out that Emily Quinn has no equal when it comes to takeoffs and landings."

"That's a little exaggerated," she told him as she stroked the heavy ball of fur that had taken up residence on her belly. "But jumps were my trademark, my signature on the ice."

"Darlin', they were more than that, I think. To quote one particularly eloquent journalist, 'She rides on a cushion of air that other skaters cannot find.'"

"You dug up that old article?" She smiled. "Although, that *was* a great quote. My granddad loved it. He said his birdhouses were responsible. They were too. They were my secret. Watching the birds taught me how to soar. For me, those few seconds in the air were the only times I felt truly in control of anything."

"I have a hard time believing that. No one gets to that level of competition without enormous self-discipline."

Emily rubbed the cat beneath his chin, letting his purr create an accompaniment to the music. "Oh, I don't have a self-disciplined bone in my body. You are sadly mistaken if you thought I called the shots in my career."

"Then who did?"

"Who didn't! My parents. Coaches. Choreographers picked my music and choreographed my routines according to the coaches' guidelines. Designers created the costumes, usually without input from me. Coaches decided when and where I would compete. Fitness consultants mapped out my strength training, and nutritionists monitored my diet. I showed up for practice. I was just the talent, the trained seal."

Gabe laughed. "So was I, darlin'."

"Oh, yeah!" Emily grinned at her unintentional pun. "I guess you were."

"We all are, one way or another. Control is just an illusion."

"Maybe it is," she agreed thoughtfully, and turned over on her side, slipping her hands beneath her cheek. Wart log-rolled as she turned and settled on her hip. "Because every time I think I've figured it out, it slips away again. When I hurt my ankle, even the illusion was gone. I lost the ability to take a world that was spinning out of control and balance it again on the edge of my blade."

"Can you skate at all anymore?"

"Oh, I can skate better than the average Joe, but without the jumps there isn't much point. Not to competing anyway." She yawned. "Are the doors locked?"

"Yes."

"Did you—"

"Checked 'em twice."

He thought she'd fallen asleep, until she hesitantly asked, "Mind if I turn on the bathroom light?"

"Go ahead."

Gabe heard her displace Wart and pick her way across the room. She flipped the switch and retraced her steps.

"'Night, Gabe."

"'Night, Emma."

Although she had turned on the bathroom light, the closet door was still wide open. Progress, Gabe thought. Not much, but progress.

Gabe rose early, driven by a sense of urgency he couldn't shake, and by the need to beat the snow predicted by early afternoon. The round trip to the cemetery was over a hundred miles, and most of Mountain Loop Highway was barely a step up from a logging road. Twenty miles out of town it turned into a narrow dirt road.

The woman occupying the passenger seat in his truck had barely spoken all morning other than to ask how cold it was and offer him Coke or coffee with his oatmeal. Right now she huddled in her parka, staring out the window as if her life depended on it.

She was mulling something over. That much was obvious. He suspected it had something to do with last night. But what?

The more he watched her, the harder she looked out the window, and the farther away she scooted. Finally he couldn't resist commenting any longer. "If you get any closer to the passenger door, you'll be riding on the outside of the truck."

Emily jumped as the sound of his voice startled her. For the past twenty minutes all she'd heard was the heater fan and the whine of the transmission as Gabe shifted gears to accommodate the road grade or icy condition. Checking her body position on the seat, she frowned.

Her knees were pressed tightly together and angled toward the door while her shoulder was jammed into the corner of the seat back and truck frame. Her right arm lay on the armrest and the fingertips of her left hand balanced on the base of the window. Gabe was right; she was practically out the door.

Anyone with half a brain would see the unusual amount of space between them and jump to the conclusion that she was afraid of him. And they'd be right. Everything about Gabe unsettled her, especially when he focused that incredibly intense gaze on her. It literally pushed heat at her. Like now.

Unzipping her parka and flapping the front, she made up an excuse for her odd behavior. "I guess I was trying to cool off. It's colder by the door."

She could tell he didn't believe a word, but he leaned over and cut the temperature lever back.

"Thanks," she said lamely.

"No problem. I was beginning to feel the heat myself." He checked the road and then let go of the wheel with one hand to shrug out of his coat. He waited until she reached out to help him before he looked her way. "I forgot how quickly two bodies can heat up a small space."

That last sentence and the warmth of his coat as she curled her fingers into the lining were Emily's wake-up call. Heat that had nothing to do with the hot air blowing out of the vents flooded her cheeks. All her life she'd been the center of people's attention, but never like this. Never like she was being savored.

Since breakfast she'd been trying to convince herself that Gabe didn't mean what he'd said last night. That he didn't want *Emma*. Did he?

In public he played the role of an enamored ex-husband: kissing her, placing his hand protectively at the small of her back, trying to rub her shoulders. He'd performed a hundred small services the previous night, exploiting anything that gave him a legitimate right to touch her. And warning off any man who so much as looked in her direction.

In private he kept his hands to himself, but he managed to touch her all the same.

Swallowing, Emily hoarsely suggested, "The road."

"Right." Gabe refocused on the road, barely avoiding a jolt to the truck but not the one to his solar plexus.

He felt like a raw recruit about to take his first rocket ride out of a C-130 plane. All a man could do was close his eyes, kiss his fear good-bye, and jump. Emma didn't look much better.

Despite the deplorable road conditions, they reached the first Darrington cemetery by nine o'clock. The spot was easy to miss, barely a dip between two forested slopes. Snow covered the ground already, the white blanket a remnant of the past week's storm. Silver firs and mountain hemlocks dotted the uneven ground and stood somber watch over the scattered graves. The tombstones resembled eerie marble petit fours, frosted with ice and snow. More ice dribbled down the sides of the monuments and glistened in the early morning sun.

A cloud scudded across the sky and cast a shadow. Emily shivered involuntarily. She'd been expecting some sort of modern cemetery with a big stone fence around it, perfectly tended grounds, and asphalt pathways. This place was none of those things. It was an old churchyard—obviously still used for burials, but isolated and tended only by love. The kind of place that cradled the history of families.

Another chill crept over her. She was about to steal the life of one of their children. That action made her feel as if she were taking on a job, a responsibility. She wondered if Gabe felt the same. She almost said something, but he shoved the truck in park and killed the engine.

After he gave the place a quick once-over for anything out the ordinary, he told her, "Let's do it."

"It seems so dishonest to take someone's name, someone's life."

"It is, but it's better than being dead. Let's go."

When she still didn't open her door, Gabe got out and wrenched it open for her. "Come on, darlin'. You know you hate not being in control of your life."

"I never said that."

"Not in so many words, but it's true. So, I'm asking you—do you want to start taking control of your life? Or do you want to sit there and give it away again?"

Stunned, Emily knew he was right. Over the years it had been easier, less risky to agree rather than take action or live with conflict. If she wasn't in control, then other people were always to blame for the bad things that happened.

Gabe might have found one of her flaws, but he also revealed the secret to maintaining control. She had to be willing to take the blame, to make the decision. That was the secret. That's why she felt in control when she jumped. She made every decision—when to take off, how fast to spin, how many revolutions, and when to land. If she fell on her butt or her face, she was responsible. She stayed in the air until she said it was over.

"I'll pick the name in a heartbeat, and I guarantee you won't like it if I do," Gabe warned her softly.

"You're right," she said. "I won't like it at all if you pick the name."

"See there? I keep telling you I'm right, but you don't listen."

"That's because you're usually yelling at me," she retorted as she swung her legs around.

"That's because you don't listen." He held out his hand to help her down. "Careful. This parking lot is a sheet of ice."

"Ice I can handle. I grew up on it," she told him as she hopped down without accepting his help. Her feet immediately slid out from under her.

Gabe caught her, dragging her back up against his chest, where his coat hung open. He gave her a minute to catch her breath, enjoying the feel of her in his arms again, enjoying the way she leaned into him so naturally. Wishing he had more time. Wishing for what he couldn't have.

Gabe drew back from the edge, but only because an icy cemetery parking lot was no place to kiss Emma. He didn't draw back completely, just far enough that something besides testosterone could influence his thinking.

"Darlin', if you handled ice any better, I'd have to carry you."

Obviously embarrassed, Emma straightened and stared at his throat. Her cheeks were flushed. "That won't be necessary. I can handle it from here."

Unfortunately she turned away from him too quickly and had to put a hand on the truck bed to steady herself.

"Right," Gabe said sarcastically.

She swung around to explain about the tennis shoes being slippery, but the excuse died on her lips. Gabe pulled a pad of paper and a gun from the glove compartment.

NINE

Gabe found the sweet spot at the small of his back and slipped the Beretta into his jeans. He hadn't intended to carry the gun until he realized the cemetery was a sniper's dream.

"Do we really need that?" Emma asked.

Slamming the truck door, Gabe said, "Probably not, but think of it as my American Express card. I don't leave home without it, and people recognize it instantly."

She didn't believe his flip answer. "It's because of the guy last night."

"It's because of a lot of things, but mostly it's common sense." Gabe switched the pad to his right hand. "Let's get this done while the mountain's out."

She followed him toward the rows of gravestones, zipping her parka and trying to find the mountain he was talking about at the same time. "Which mountain? They're all around us."

"None of these slopes. It's an expression I learned

growing up in Seattle, a way of announcing the day is beautiful. Mt. Rainier is usually hidden by clouds near the top of Crystal Mountain. So around Seattle, when the mountain is out—"

"It's a clear day."

"You got it."

They trudged through wet snow toward a side area where the markers looked newer and a few granite benches were scattered beneath the trees. Every few steps, Emily found herself glancing over her shoulder. Something about being in the graveyard unnerved her. Maybe it was Gabe's gun.

To take her mind off the surroundings, Emily tried to make conversation. "So the orphanage you mentioned, the one with the nuns, that was in Seattle?"

"Yep." Gabe walked more slowly, reading the epitaphs as he went.

Emily looked over her shoulder again, hating the sound of crusted snow crunching beneath their shoes. She didn't watch horror movies, and she didn't like quiet, scary places. "So . . . tell me about it. Every detail."

"There's not much to tell. St. Christopher's Home for Children is run by nuns. It's a big gray stone building with a courtyard near the waterfront."

God, she hated economical conversationalists. "Sounds pretty."

"Hardly. The place is falling down around their wimples."

"Why not sell?"

"They should. They could make a fortune, but they don't listen to me."

Surprised, Emily said, "Somehow I got the impression that you didn't keep in contact with them."

"I don't," he answered absently, and hunkered down to brush a snowdrift away from the base so he could get a better look at the dates. "The last time I saw Sister Mary Joseph was when I paid my bill."

"Your bill?" Emily asked, puzzled by his choice of words.

Gabe's hand stilled as he realized what he'd said. A second later he brushed the last of the snow away from the date and ignored her question. "If you don't object to being thirty, this one might do."

"Fine. Put her down as a possible. When I'm sixty I'll look young for my age. Now back up. When did nuns start running a tab on charity?"

Gabe sighed and looked up. He could tell that Emily wasn't going to let go of this, and he kicked himself for opening the door. "Nuns don't run a tab on charity. They give it away free."

The bitter edge in his voice was the only clue Emily needed. "But you don't take charity," she surmised as he stared at her. "You pay your debts, your *bills*."

"That's right." He stood up.

"And that's why Patrick was so certain you'd honor the dog tag. Not just because he saved your life, but because you hate to owe anyone anything."

He didn't confirm or deny her off-the-cuff psychological analysis. Instead, he walked toward the next headstone. "We need several names to make sure we get one that hasn't been issued a social security number. And to make sure we get a kid that was actually born in Washington State. Thank God no one was routinely fingerprinting for identification twenty-odd years ago. That's one less thing I have to worry about."

Emily almost laughed when she realized why he was suddenly so talkative. The man was trying to steer the focus away from himself. She didn't take the bait.

Instead, she kept going over something Marsha Jean had said that first night. Something about not having to cut any of his trees for money. And then the significance hit her.

"You're a man who pays his debts. Is that why you have a hard time making payroll? You give a lot of your money to the nuns to pay them back for raising you?"

"No. I have a hard time making payroll because there aren't enough people bending elbows in my bar."

"Don't you get a pension or something?"

He turned on her. "Aren't you being kind of personal?"

"You're asking me to put my life in your hands. Don't you think I'm entitled to know a little something about you?" she asked. "Like what kind of man you are?"

Gabe narrowed his eyes and walked away. "I opted out early. No pension, but I do all right."

"Patrick said you *retired.* So even leaving early you should have gotten a lump sum or—" She stopped and stared at his back. "You gave it all to them."

He kept walking. "No."

She hurried to catch up; making her way through a slushy patch of snow in cheap tennis shoes was like walking through wet sand. "Most of it, then."

"No." Halting suddenly, he whipped around and told her the truth to end the ridiculous guessing game.

"I gave them half of it. The rest was a down payment on the bar and my cabin—I use the term loosely—outside town. Can we drop this now?"

Emily got the message and nodded. They marched off down the row again. "Bet they were proud," she said softly. She thought what he did for the nuns was wonderful, but she knew he'd be mad at her for not letting it go.

Closing his eyes, Gabe ground his teeth and exhaled a breath. Emma didn't get it. She was raised in a different world. "No, they were not proud. *Parents* are proud. Sister Mary Joseph was grateful."

"How do you know she doesn't feel like a parent?"

"Because she threw me out of the orphanage the day I turned eighteen," he said as he wrote down yet another name on the pad.

"See there," Emily said. "That proves my point."

"And how the hell do you figure that?" Gabe threw up his hands, amazed that he was even having this conversation with her. He'd never let anyone dig around in his past like this.

"Mother birds always nudge the baby chicks out of the nest."

Gabe laughed. "I'm not a chick, and it wasn't a nudge. It was a good swift kick. Plain and simple. She needed the bed."

"Maybe that's just what you were supposed to think. By kicking you out she made sure that you'd go out into the world and not look back."

"Now, why would you make that assumption?" he asked with deadly calm. He hid his emotions perfectly, but instinct told Emily that she was on very shaky ground.

"W-well," she began, putting her hands in her pockets as she defended her position. "I assumed she knew how you felt about taking charity, and paying your debts, and being responsible. Maybe she wanted to give you a chance to find your own place in the world without having to worry about your obligations to them."

He tapped the pad against his thigh and shook his head. "Guilt is a nun's stock-in-trade. They are experts at twisting the screws, so your version doesn't make sense."

"It does if she loved you, and I think she probably did—" Emily stumbled as she realized how easy it would be to love Gabe. He needed someone to love him. A split second later, she wondered if Gabe had ever truly allowed himself to love anyone.

She plunged ahead before she could think about that anymore. "She probably *does* love you, and you should thank her. She knows you can't chain someone to you by need. It's much harder to love someone and let them go."

"On which idiot talk show did you hear that theory?"

"Not a talk show, just personal experience," she said bluntly. "That's what my parents did. They chained me with guilt and made me chase their dream in the name of love. I never got to stand on my own two feet because they were afraid I wouldn't choose to stand atop an Olympic medal platform."

"Were they right?" he asked, zeroing in on the issue she had barely begun to admit to herself.

"We'll never know now," she lied, and flicked a glance at his pad. "Do we have enough names?"

"Not yet."

"Hurry up. Being here gives me the creeps," Emily confessed irritably. "I don't need any reminders about death right now, or the past, or what it feels like to be alone."

"You're not alone," Gabe pointed out.

"I don't mean alone here. I mean *alone*. I think that's what scares me most in this whole mess. My parents and grandparents are dead, but I had cousins, an elderly aunt in a nursing home. I had family, you know? Suddenly because of this mess, they're gone too, and I *am* alone."

Gabe stopped abruptly in front of a monument topped by a stone angel. "Darlin', family comes in two flavors—blood and chosen. Starting over doesn't mean you can't make a new family. It doesn't take away your memories. I don't even have those."

"How did your parents die?"

"I don't know if they have." He looked away for a moment, as if making a decision. While he studied the trees in the distance, he said, "I was driven to a strange city and abandoned on a street corner. My mother said she'd be right back, and then she got as far away from me as she could."

Emily's heart contracted at the hard edge in Gabe's voice, and her jaw tightened with anger at the woman who'd abandoned him. "How old were you?"

"Six."

Shocked she gaped. "Six! She left you on a corner? How could a mother do that? Something could have happened to you!"

"It did." Gabe pulled his attention from the trees and looked at her. "I got sent to the orphanage."

"She must have known that," Emily offered, latching on to the first plausible justification. "Surely she believed you'd be adopted?"

"Not likely. Six-year-old boys who don't talk don't usually get adopted."

"You couldn't talk and she left you in a strange city?"

"Not *couldn't. Wouldn't.* Not until I was ten. I was an 'elective mute.' A real hard case for the orphanage. Nuns ran my life until I was eighteen, and then the navy took over."

Emily's blood ran cold as she realized that being abandoned at six might have been the least of Gabe's childhood traumas. She tried not to visualize the circumstances that would make not talking a safer choice for a child than talking.

"How'd they know your name? Could you write?"

"No. Sister named me," he said, but this time Emily thought she heard a grudging respect for the sister if not affection. "Don't remember my real name anymore. When I showed up at the orphanage, Sister kept asking me if I had a Christian name, and I kept nodding my head to tell her that I did. She finally took all that nodding to mean that my Christian name was Christian."

Smiling, Emily said, "Of course. That makes perfect sense, as does Gabriel. I assume she chose it too?"

"Oh, yeah. For a lot of reasons. Not the least of which was to remind me that one day I would want to blow my horn."

"Sounds like a wise lady."

"Wise enough. She knew that if there was any hope of my making it through this world in one piece, I was going to need a guardian angel."

The archangel Gabriel. Emily closed her eyes and felt a fresh stab of guilt for the secret she kept.

Don't tell the Archangel I caught a bullet. He thinks I'm invincible. Patrick wasn't delusional. His last words were for Gabe. One last jest between friends.

"Archangel," she whispered.

"Patrick calls me that," Gabe said distractedly, looking into the distance.

"I know. He told me." *Chosen, not blood, but brothers all the same,* Emily realized.

She wished she'd never started this conversation. Sharing pieces of their lives was dangerous. Understanding created bonds that weren't easily cast off. Like now. She felt the weight of the secret she carried so intensely because she'd broken the golden rule—*Never trust anyone.* But she trusted Gabe. She trusted him to protect her.

Now all that trust was backfiring, forcing her to tell him the truth about Patrick. Whatever happened afterward was his call, but she couldn't let him risk his life with that secret between them. Patrick deserved better. Gabe deserved better.

"Gabe, I need to talk—"

"Don't say a word. Don't look around. Just walk over here behind this monument."

"What?"

"Don't argue, Emma. Just do it. We've got company on the ridge." When she froze, Gabe pulled his gun, never taking his eyes off the heavily wooded crest. "If you don't move now, I'll shoot you myself."

As he intended, his comment and his action were enough to shock her out of the paralyzing fear that kept her rooted in place. Unfortunately Emma's instinct for survival kicked in like Thor's hammer. She practically dove behind the memorial in her haste to obey.

"That was certainly subtle," Gabe said as her body slammed into his. He made room for her by sliding to the left. "Let's hope our boy's sight picture was blurred at that moment. Otherwise, he knows we know."

"How do you know for sure? I can't see anything but trees. So how can you see something that far away?"

Gabe appreciated the fact that the lady didn't fall apart. He could deal with momentary panic. He could answer questions, but hysteria would have gotten them both killed.

"The sun's striking something over there that flashes a reflection," he explained. "Whatever it is, it's moving. Up and to the north of us. My guess is a rifle scope."

Emma heaved a sigh of relief. "Oh, thank God. I thought you saw a person. If it's a rifle, then it's probably a hunter like at Marsha Jean's."

"Not likely." Gabe concentrated, trying to calculate the distance from the ridge to the monument. Looked like a couple hundred yards. Tough shot for anyone but a pro. "Ain't nothin' in season on that ridge but us."

"How do you know that?" He could hear the disappointment and challenge in her voice.

"Because our Uncle Sam owns that particular piece of real estate."

"Oh, my God. It can't be. Not now. Not when I'm so close. How the hell did they find me?"

"You tell me, darlin'. You laid the trail; you dropped the bread crumbs."

"But I didn't. I was careful. I rented three cars and ditched them all around Boise. I ditched . . . the marshal's car. I got the habit in a costume shop from a seventeen-year-old who never once looked up from his chemistry book." She grabbed a handful of his jacket, clutching it until her knuckles were white. "I bought a piece garbage car from a guy so shady he had moss on his shoes. They did not follow *me.*"

Not bothering to remove her hand, Gabe surveyed the landscape again. "Well, I beg to differ, Emma. They followed something, but they wouldn't want to kill you in town. Too many witnesses. It'd be days before anyone found the bodies out here."

"But how did they follow us *here* without you seeing them?"

"Transmitter on my truck would be my guess. He tracked us, and now he's going for position."

Something's wrong with this, Gabe thought uneasily. A pro wouldn't set up a shot like this—not one through a loose maze of trees in a cemetery full of tombstones, which made excellent cover for his targets. So, what's he up to? Gabe felt the adrenaline boost his senses as he marked the last spot he saw the light flash and then the truck in the parking lot.

"He wants to drop us at the truck," he said suddenly. "Figures he can get us both quick, with the first two shots. Fewer trees in the way. No maze of angels and granite memorials to mess up his shot. Yardage is a little shorter too. Not much, but enough to up his odds. And he won't have to leave that heavy cover to do it."

Emma pulled away finally. She shivered and huddled in her parka. "What do we do now?"

"*We* don't do much of anything. You keep your head down and your feet ready. I'll take care of the problem."

"How?"

"Any way I can."

Gabe ignored the cold radiating from the frozen ground. Nor did he dwell on the discomfort caused by crouching in one position for far too long. The only thoughts he allowed himself were the ones that began with "what if?"

What if there were two of them?

What if he couldn't approach without alerting the sniper?

What if the sun didn't catch the scope again?

The game was Gabe's personal version of twenty questions. Every conceivable scenario played quietly in his head while he waited for the sun to kiss the scope again and give him a location. When it flashed, the glint came from a spot slightly below a trio of ancient cedars. Gabe smiled. He had the bastard now.

Before he moved, he glanced down at the cemetery. If the sniper wanted her, he was going to have to find a way to put a bullet through two feet of solid granite. Nothing of her could be seen from there, not the top of her head, not a shoulder, not a foot. Satisfied that Emma was scared enough or smart enough to hold tight, Gabe began to work his way around and above the cedars.

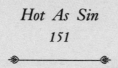

Emily didn't ordinarily believe in omens, but it was hard to ignore the obvious.

The stone angel above her had broken wingtips and the battle scars of vandalism. From her perspective on the ground, flaws like that should have been easy to miss. Instead, the imperfections jumped out at her—a warning that no one was immune from violence. Nothing was sacred. Not holy symbols, and certainly not human life.

Violence fed on itself and played by no one's rules. It caught hold of people and wouldn't let go until the urge to protect dissolved into the need to attack. The one slowly becoming the other.

Like now.

She wasn't running. She was cornered. The only way to survive was to attack. Protecting her meant Gabe had to complete the circle of violence.

Emily tried to ignore the cold, but she couldn't. It was all around her. In the ground, in the granite, and in her heart.

As she shifted, the sound of a shot drove the cold deep into her soul.

TEN

When the shot rang out, Gabe abandoned his careful, silent assault. His only concern was to prevent the second shot, in case the first one hadn't torn through her.

Why didn't you stay down, Emma? Dammit, why didn't you do what I told you to do?

Heedless of the sting of icy evergreen needles, he practically slid the last fifty feet into the sniper's base. A split second was all Gabe needed to let his concern for Emma fade and focus on the shooter. Time stretched, drawing out his actions in slow motion, a feeling that was so familiar to Gabe.

The shooter was about forty and carefully dressed in a hunter's worn-out camouflage coverall and flapped hat. Surprise registered on his face as he turned his head, but not the rifle, toward Gabe. Surprise matured into fear, and the sniper's hands convulsed on the high-powered rifle too late. There wasn't enough time to bring it around or change his position to get the shot.

"Don't," Gabe ordered. "Scoot away from it. On your belly."

"All right. All right. I didn't do anything."

"Shut up." Gabe risked a glance in Emma's direction. He couldn't see much from this distance.

His gaze swung back to the man on the ground and registered the detail he'd completely missed. The guy's rifle wasn't aimed at the cemetery. Gabe didn't like what he was thinking. Not at all. Odds were, he'd caught a poacher and not a sniper.

"What the hell were you shooting at?"

"Nothing." The word was muffled against the ground. "I didn't hit anything. I was just practicing with my new scope."

"That so? You're either incompetent or a liar or both."

Walking closer, Gabe knelt down—the Beretta ready in his hand. The shooter—still on his belly—was silent, determined to play the tough guy.

"So which are you? Incompetent or a liar?"

"You a ranger?"

"No."

"Then why the hell do you care what I shoot?"

"I'm funny that way." He checked the rifle, the scope, and the ammo. Then he looked at his man on the ground. "What kind of hunter carries this much firepower?"

By the time Emily heard Gabe holler her name, she had made so many promises to God that she couldn't remember them all. Most of them were about keeping

Gabe safe. She hadn't worried about escaping or whether the man with the rifle would close in to pick her off. What she had worried about was Gabe's life.

Something inside her had broken when she heard the shot.

"It's okay, Emma," he called again.

Relief surged through her, burning away the cold as she let go of the fear. She scrambled up as fast as her stiffened muscles would let her and peered over the monument base. Gabe casually pointed a rifle at a man who marched in front of him. Standing all the way up, she took her first full breath in half an hour.

The only thing stopping her from running to him was the fact that her legs wouldn't move. She'd never been more thankful to see anyone in her entire life. As they got closer, she tried to spot bloodstains or any sign of weakness.

"I heard the shot. I thought—I was sure—"

"Nothing is ever sure, Emma. Which is why I'd like to introduce you to Joe Honeycutt. You can stop right there, Joe. Is he the one?"

Emily studied him, trying to find any feature that struck a chord. But there was none of the apprehension she'd felt in the bar. None of the recognition. Unexpectedly, a crushing disappointment filled her. The horrible waiting, Gabe's risk, it had all been for nothing.

"No. It's not him."

"Didn't think it was." Gabe lowered the rifle. "But I couldn't take a chance."

Joe turned, dropping his hands but not his voice. "You are a lunatic!"

"Maybe, but I've got the gun."

Joe settled himself down, moderating his voice. "I told you the lady wouldn't know me. Give me my stuff like you promised."

Gabe tossed him a wallet, which he caught with one hand. "I don't think I can give you the rifle."

"You don't think you can— Do you know what that piece cost? What the scope cost?"

"Almost to the penny." Gabe motioned for Emily to circle around and come to his side. "You want it back, Joe? Check at the police station in Rock Falls. You can claim it there. As a favor, I'll report having found it leaning against a tree."

"How the hell am I going to explain how I lost a rifle?"

"I don't know," Gabe said with what sounded like genuine concern. "Would it be easier if I took you to the ranger's station? How much explanation do you think they'll need?"

That shut Joe up long enough for Emily to ask, "What's going on?"

Gabe systematically ejected the cartridges from the rifle. "Mr. Honeycutt is loaded for bear. Literally. Black bear. There's a certain internal organ that's a prized Oriental medicine component. Worth a thousand dollars. Then there's the pelt and the meat."

"He shot a bear? You mean he's not—"

"No," Gabe interrupted before she could say anything more. "He's not. He's just a bad shot with too much gun. Damn bear was probably groggy as hell, waking up just long enough to forage for food, and Joe here missed him anyway." Gabe handed her the rifle and pulled his Beretta. "Go away, Mr. Honeycutt. My wife has a fondness for bears. I don't want to keep her upset over this mess."

The hunter was red with rage, but walked away. "I don't know who the hell you think you are."

"A concerned citizen."

Gabe put his arm around Emily. She didn't object. She needed some reassurance after that morning's emotional roller coaster, and she doubted he'd ever offer again. Not after she told him about Patrick. Later, she promised, later, when she was calmer. When they were home.

After Honeycutt disappeared into the trees, she shivered. The cemetery, surrounded by the wilderness, was too quiet again. Honeycutt might have been harmless, but he was a reminder nevertheless that she was someone's prey. A hunter was stalking, a hunter who wanted her dead.

"Are we through?" she asked. Emily pulled the pad out of her pocket and handed it to Gabe.

"No," he said, an odd expression on his face. He lowered his head until his lips met hers. Awareness rushed through her, a chain reaction of feeling that erased the last of the numbness inside her. The kiss was deep and hard and quick.

Gabe pulled away and said, "We're not through, but we can go."

Neither of them spoke much on the way back to Rock Falls. Gabe thought Emma needed some time to come to terms with what had happened in the cemetery.

This time they were lucky, but they both knew that luck ran out eventually.

True to his word, he stopped by the police station to turn in the rifle. "This will only take a minute," he promised. "I'll tell 'em why I'm here and then come back for the rifle."

"Take as long as you need. I'm fine."

Gabe didn't believe that for a minute. Her voice was hollow, as if she operated on automatic. Her eyes totally confused him though. Fear, even terror, he expected to see, but not guilt. Once more he promised, "I won't be long."

The station was a little busier than yesterday, but not much. Willis was pointing out something in a folder to another officer. He handed the file off and waved Gabe over. "What brings you back so soon? Another rock?"

"No, my luck's changing. I found a rifle in the woods up by my cabin. Expensive gun, with a scope to die for. I'm hoping no one will claim it."

Willis snorted and finger-combed one of his sideburns. "Some rich hunter laid it up beside the tree and forgot it. He'll be calling every official between here and Tacoma."

"That's what I figured too. I've got it out in the truck. Didn't want to surprise you guys by walking in with a rifle. I've found out I don't like being shot at in my old age."

Looking around him, Willis spotted Emma in the truck. He straightened and grinned at Gabe, a sly grin. "That's not all you got in that truck. Who is the babe?"

Gabe didn't like his tone and didn't like the way he leered. "Emma Gabriel. My not-so-ex-wife."

"Message received." Willis laughed and threw his hands up in a mock attempt to push Gabe back. "Bring her in. I'd like to meet her."

"She's shy."

"She'll be frozen by the time we finish with the paperwork. Come on." Willis's words were softly spoken, more invitation than order. "Bring her in."

Gabe knew he'd made a tactical error. He should have dropped Emma at the bar first, but he hadn't wanted to leave her alone that long. Their "couple" cover was designed to fool people who really didn't care. Willis, on the other hand, was in the business of turning over rocks just to see what was under them. Trotting their act out in front of him would be like putting a show on Broadway without a rehearsal.

In this situation he didn't have much choice but to raise the curtain.

"I'll ask her," Gabe told him.

"No, no." Willis clapped him on the shoulder and walked out to the truck with him. "*I'll* ask her. Then she can't say no."

The wiry young officer strolled out of the police station right behind Gabe, clapping him on the back and laughing at a joke of some kind. As soon as she saw the officer, Emily choked back a giggle and thought, *Oh, my God. Elvis lives!*

The urge to laugh faded the moment the officer approached the truck and gave her an oddly confident smile. By then she could see his eyes—blacker than dark brown but still not jet black. They seemed out of place and much too old for a cop several years younger than she. His face smiled, but those eyes didn't. Those eyes were busy picking her apart and alarmed her much more than the stiff frown on Gabe's face.

Gabe hauled open the door and nodded approval to the other man, who opened her door. "Emma, this is Derick Willis, one of Rock Falls' finest. I'm going to have to answer some questions about the rifle, and he was afraid you'd be too cold out here."

"Yes, ma'am." Derick leaned an arm casually against the edge of the door and held out his hand to help her down. "We couldn't have a fatality in the parking lot of the station. You come on in, and I'll get you a cup of coffee while you wait."

Without Gabe having to tell her, Emily knew to tread carefully with this cop. Nothing she said would completely erase the suspicion she saw in the officer's gaze. It seemed a natural part of the man, just like the badge. But the right attitude would soften his suspicion and turn it into simple curiosity. So "Emma" heaved a great big sigh of relief and threw herself at Derick as she scrambled out of the truck.

"Oh, thank you. I am so glad there is at least one man in this town who has the guts to stand up to Gabe. God knows why I married him, but the reason I divorced him is coming back to me." She spared a displeased look at Gabe—making sure Derick had a good view of the way her lip curled. "It was plain and simple jealousy."

"Was it?" Derick shot Gabe a speculative glance. "I

never figured Gabe for the jealous type. I never figured Gabe for the marrying kind either. He told me once he was a confirmed bachelor."

Bingo, Emily thought. That's why Derick was so pushy about her coming in. He'd caught Gabe in a lie.

"Ha!" she exploded, aiming her comment at Gabe. "Doesn't that just figure. If the man had his way, he wouldn't mention me to anyone. He'd keep me locked up in a room somewhere." She crooked her finger for Derick to come closer, and prayed that Gabe would do his part. "The man is positively stone-henged."

"That's *stone-aged*," Gabe snarled at her. "Stone-aged. If you're going to insult me, then at least get it right."

"Whatever." Emily waved off his correction as if this were a longstanding argument.

Gabe grabbed the rifle and slammed the truck door. Looking pointedly at Derrick, he said, "See? And you wonder why I divorced her?"

"No, sir." As Derick shut her door, he was smiling again, but this time it was with enjoyment. He liked seeing Gabe in a situation the former SEAL couldn't handle. "I'm wondering why she married you."

Emily circled her arm in Derick's and tossed a victorious smirk in Gabe's direction. He was waiting, and none too patiently, by the station door. She intended to add one last touch to her performance as the talkative, outspoken Emma Gabriel. But the performance ended as soon as she met his hungry gaze.

The attraction that was always between them, always lurking beneath the surface, flared to life. Her easy smile faltered, then disappeared completely as she realized her emotions went beyond sexual attraction. Gabe easily had as many flaws as he had virtues. Right now he was the only thing real in her life. The only person she could trust.

"Look at him," she said softly, covering her confusion with the flip personality of Emma Gabriel. "How could a girl not marry him?"

Derick grinned at Gabe's discomfort. "Mrs. Gabriel, I certainly like having you around."

With that pronouncement of approval, the subject of their relationship seemed to have been satisfactorily covered. After the introductions around the squad room, Emily faded into the background. Taking her coffee from Derick with a murmured thank-you, she sat quietly in the extra chair he'd dragged over to his desk.

Questions about the rifle were short and simple. The coffee was surprisingly good. No one at the station paid any attention to her. And she paid very little attention to them until Derick dropped the bomb.

"That's it on the rifle, Gabe, but I thought you'd want to know I got another report from my buddy. He's still working with the marshals on that disappearance. Rubbing it in every chance he gets."

Shock caused Emily's throat to constrict, and she choked on a mouthful of coffee. Both men swiveled to check on her as she grabbed a napkin and wiped her mouth. Gabe put his hand on her arm and squeezed gently as a warning while he made a production of banging her on the back. "You okay?"

Coughing and her eyes watering, she nodded. "Just went down the wrong way. Sorry," she rasped. "Go on.

I'm fine." She was anything but fine, but she tried not to show it.

Derick leaned back in his chair. His gaze stayed on her long enough to make her uncomfortable. Finally he looked back at Gabe. "Well, there's another little wrinkle. Something that happened before the pro turned up missing. Seems they've misplaced a witness. They got two marshals down at a safe house. Both dead. One of 'em went down hard."

Emily held her coffee cup tightly with both hands, trying to steady it. A wave of nausea hit her as she silently pleaded, *Not this way. Don't let it be this way.* Gabe would never forgive her if he found out this way.

"Two marshals down?" Gabe asked with a whistle. He let go of her arm, and leaned back in his chair too. "No wonder the Justice Department is pushing on this one. Sort of makes them all look like the boy wonder on a bad day. Who went down? Surely not experienced men?"

Why hadn't she told him in the cemetery? Because it wasn't the place. There was too much death there already, too much fear. Not that her reasons would matter now. It was too late. Emily closed her eyes and waited for her lies to unravel.

"Nobody's saying who they are," Derick said, "but how green could the guys have been? You don't pull witness security detail if you're fresh off the farm."

For a few seconds the words made no sense at all, and then they suddenly clicked. Relief rushed through Emily so fast, the room swam. She had to fight a sigh. Derick didn't know! He couldn't tell Gabe.

"No, Justice doesn't like 'em green," Gabe agreed. "They like a little mileage on their men."

"Well, they don't like mileage on their witnesses and this one seems to have put the pedal to the metal. Popular opinion is that she's still alive. She's a rabbit going to ground."

"Say a few prayers and maybe she'll hop toward Washington and you can snare her."

"No such luck, man. For the foreseeable future I'm filing reports and writing tickets. If it comes to that, they'll call in the county mounties. Not me."

Gabe got up. "Come on by the bar tonight. I'll buy you a drink to cheer you up."

"Just might do that. I want to have a chat with Sawyer Johns and Clayton Dover. A friendly chat." Derick turned and nodded at her. "Pleasure to meet you, Mrs. Gabriel."

"Oh, call me Emma, please." She struggled to pull herself together. She couldn't blow it now. "All my friends call me Emma. Come to think of it—only women call me Emma. I don't have any male friends, because no man has ever survived Gabe's screening process. Maybe you could be the first?"

"He's not interested, Emma," Gabe informed her.

"Sec! The man is a ne'er-do-well."

"Neanderthal," Gabe corrected her. "Ne-an-der-thal."

Emily waved at him. "Whatever."

Gabe groaned and dragged her by the arm. "We're leaving now. Say good-bye, Emma."

"Oh, sure. I find a new friend, and suddenly we're leaving! See? Bye, Derick!"

She let herself be hauled toward the door, but another argument erupted before they got out the door, continuing unabated until they'd pulled away from the station.

"Not bad, Mrs. Gabriel," Gabe said as they turned the corner. "Not bad at all. We might survive this yet."

Emily let her head rest against the seat, a strange exhilaration welling up inside her. "I can't believe I was in a police station, talking about *me*, and they didn't even know."

"Safest place to hide is in plain sight."

Straightening up, Emily shoved her hair back from her face. "Why didn't you tell me you'd gone to pump him for information? And what was he talking about? Why am I *another* wrinkle?"

"Yesterday, all he knew was that Joseph Bookman disappeared in transit."

"W-what?" Emily held herself very still, as if that would change his answer to something she liked better.

"My guess is that when the marshals found out about the farmhouse, they tried to move Bookman. Or that Bookman found out that the attempt on you failed; probably figured he was next. So he struck a deal, and they moved him for security. Whoever got to you probably had the juice to get to Bookman even in jail. The only question seems to be whether or not Bookman's dead." He paused. "No bodies have turned up."

"And that's bad?" Emily asked, knowing in her heart that it was.

"Yeah. If Bookman's not dead, he's looking for you too."

"He won't stop until he finds me. Will he?"

"No."

She tried not to let it bother her. What was one more gun pointed in her direction? Seemed like everyone had a gun. Everyone wanted to kill her.

Emily stared out the window. It bothered her. It terrified her. And so did what she had to do next. She had to tell Gabe.

When the bar loomed in front of them, the liquor distributor's truck was backing up to leave. Gabe wheeled into the parking lot and jumped out almost before they stopped rolling. In the end he had to bribe the guy into hanging around long enough to unload. He was obsessively attached to his schedule, and Gabe had already kept him waiting fifteen minutes.

Emily left Gabe to deal with the driver and disappeared upstairs. She paced until her gaze found the mess of files on Gabe's desk. To give herself something to do with her hands, she began straightening pages that stuck out of the folders at every angle imaginable. Each time the steps creaked, she caught her breath, afraid that the time had come to face Gabe and confess. When Wart jumped off the pool table onto the floor behind her, she startled so badly, the file went flying out of her hands, scattering papers everywhere.

"Oh, damn. Now see what you've done?" she asked him as she knelt down to gather up the pages. Wart kept butting his head against her hands, oblivious of the havoc he'd caused. "I am not in the mood for this, cat. He's going to be mad enough. These are his supplier faxes, and they're all dated, which means I've got to put them back in order before—"

The document in her hand was dated the day she'd

arrived, and it was addressed not to a supplier but to Patrick.

Who was already dead before the fax was sent.

She read it twice, telling herself that it was coincidence. That Gabe never really sent it, or the special Christmas present he mentioned was a set of golf clubs or maybe a microwave for Patrick's mother—*any* present that would be tough to wrap. But there wasn't a present in sight.

Only her.

She wasn't certain how long she sat there before she heard Gabe's familiar footfall on the stairs. She was certain, however, that the only man she could trust couldn't be trusted at all.

No one could.

Her parents had wanted a child only so they could shape and mold her into an Olympic gold medalist, a dream they hadn't been able to achieve for themselves. Her coaches had used her talent to launch careers. Her corporate sponsors wanted her face, but at least they had offered to pay for the privilege. The government wanted her as leverage. Everyone had an agenda.

Thank God she hadn't made the mistake of letting her emotions toward Gabe get out of hand. Falling in love with him would have given him another weapon he could use to control her.

When he reached the threshold, she didn't get up. She held out the fax.

"What the hell have you done, Gabe?"

ELEVEN

Words died on Gabe's lips as his mind registered the scene in front of him. Emma knelt on the floor by his desk, papers everywhere. Betrayal and fear fought for control of her expression as she waited.

He didn't bother to ask for the piece of paper in her hand; he knew what she held. It was just as well. Tomorrow morning he would have had to tell her anyway. Pitching his keys on the coffee table, he said, "I sent Patrick a fax. Even on assignment he checks in once or twice a week."

"It's true," she whispered, knowing she should have expected Gabe to do something like this. "Someone in his office knows I'm here."

"No, they don't." He hated the raw emotion he saw on her face. "Look at the fax. My telephone number isn't on it. I took the sender code off. I didn't sign the damn thing. I routed it through an oil company in New York. No one's going to pay attention to an obviously personal fax. *No one* but Patrick could possibly know you're here or what that fax means!"

Emily reined in her fear. Right now she needed to think more than she needed to feel. Letting the fax slide out of her fingers, she said, "You never intended to help me. You've been scurrying around behind my back the whole time. Checking up on my story. First with this fax and then by going to the police yesterday. You didn't care about your promise."

"That's not true," he said heavily, and crossed the room to help her up.

Emily jerked away from his touch, forcing herself to get up under her own power. The physical contact destroyed the emotional distance she'd been trying so hard to maintain. His touch fed the fire of betrayal inside her, reminding her that the only one she could count on was herself.

"You lied to me. You promised you wouldn't contact him. You said you owed him enough to take the dog tag on faith. Oops," she corrected herself sarcastically, and put the pool table between them. "I forgot. You have a little problem with faith. You were never very good at it."

"I warned you," he ground out.

"You did. I just didn't listen." She exhaled the words on a breath that was full of self-ridicule. "I didn't know you that first night, and afterward I thought you were different. Guess not! Guess I'm never going to learn. I'm just going to keep trusting people and getting shafted."

"Hold on. I had good reason to send him that fax."

Gabe's words were soft but laced with anger barely held in check.

"Of course you did." Her head snapped up, her tone just as righteous as his had been, but not nearly as restrained. "Not the least of which is your need to be in control of every situation. Like today in the cemetery, when you went after that poor hunter and scared him half to death."

"This has nothing to do with control, Emma. Not the way you think anyway." He had his hands on his hips. His gaze never wavered. "Two days ago I didn't know you. The debt I owed was to Patrick. Not to you. I did what I thought he wanted."

"You didn't have to think! I told you what he wanted—he wanted you to help me disappear! No questions."

"Listen to me, Emma. I thought he wanted me to slow you down. I thought he needed me to buy him some time, to baby-sit you until he broke loose from his assignment." He flared his fingers, digging them into the denim as he spoke. "I figured he was going to come get you. That was the only explanation for the clues he had you drop."

Frozen in place, Emily couldn't believe what she was hearing. "Come get me? Clues? There weren't any clues."

"Sorry, darlin', but there were. Lots of them."

"Like what?" she asked, dreading the answer.

"Patrick never gives advice. Ever. That was your first mistake, saying that it would be safer to take his advice. Then there's the fact that the word 'safe' is not in his vocabulary. He wouldn't use it. Even the nun's habit was classic Patrick Talbot. It screamed 'look but don't touch,' especially to someone raised by nuns, as I was."

"The habit was my idea," she broke in.

"I know that now, but *then* I thought it was Patrick's idea of a joke. He has this talent for practical jokes. And the last clue—the real clincher—is that Patrick would never tell me to 'forget' you if he actually wanted you to disappear. That's like telling me how to breathe. It goes without saying."

"Patrick never intended any of that," she explained slowly, her heart racing at the mess Gabe's cleverness had created.

"You're right. He never intended you to use that dog tag. Never in a million years. He's full of grand gestures, and giving you the tag was one of them. Believe me, he had no idea that things were going to go to hell in a hand basket and that you'd end up on my doorstep."

"Yes, he did." A coldness settled around Emily's heart and in her stomach. She and Gabe were both at fault for this, and she was as much to blame as Gabe for trying to control the situation. Maybe more so.

"How could he have known?"

"He knew."

Despite the distance between them, Gabe saw the glitter of unshed tears, heard the regret in her words. The hair on the back of his neck stood up. "Emma, that doesn't answer my question." Very slowly, very carefully, he repeated, "How could he have known?"

"I'm so sorry, Gabe," she whispered, and paused, pressing her lips together the way people did when they didn't want to cry. Her chin quivered and one fat tear slid down her cheek and rolled off her jaw.

For the first time in his life Gabe's knees actually buckled. He put his hands on the table to steady himself, her silence killing him. He didn't yell, but his words blasted her nonetheless. *"How could he know?"*

"Because he gave me the dog tag before he died!" she shouted, losing the battle with her tears, hating him for making her say it like this, hating herself all over again for having left Patrick. "Do you get it now, Gabe? I left him alone in that farmhouse. With no one to hold his hand or tell him it was going to be all right. I was too much of a coward to stay. He sent me here because I had nowhere else to go, and he was dying."

Gabe sucked in a breath and let it out slowly as he rocked back and forth over the pool table, trying to control the pain that burned its way to the spot in his soul where he kept his feelings for Patrick. It wasn't possible. It couldn't be. Not Patrick. Not this way. And then the iron grip he normally had on his emotions deserted him as he realized that the funeral had come and gone, and he hadn't been there to say good-bye.

Picking up the eight ball, he tested its weight and flung it at the wall, not caring that Emily flinched and ducked. Plaster cracked and shattered under the impact, dusting the floor with white powder. The ball hit the floor hard with a deadened thump and rolled to a stop beside Wart, who lay on the scattered papers, his ears flattened.

Without another word Gabe walked away and stared out the window at the light snow drifting down.

Frightened more of the silence than of his anger,

Emily wrapped her arms around her midriff, uncertain what to say, wishing she could change what had happened. The pain on Gabe's face was almost more than she could bear, especially now that she knew him, knew his past. Patrick had been his brother. *Chosen*, not blood, but family all the same. She understood that now, but it was too late to undo the damage.

"I was afraid you'd want revenge," she explained softly, knowing something had to be said. "I was afraid you'd use me as bait to get it."

Gabe didn't turn away from the window. "So you used me instead."

"I didn't have a choice!"

"Everyone has a choice, Emma."

"Two days ago I didn't know you any more than you knew me. I had no way of telling whether you'd honor a promise to a dead man. I was terrified. For God's sake, someone was trying to kill me! *I didn't know you.* You were just a name, somewhere to run."

When Gabe finally looked at her, a fresh wave of loss swamped him. He could count the people he cared about on two fingers. One of them was dead, and the other was explaining in great detail what he already knew. She saw him as a protector, someone to get her through the crisis. Someone to leave behind when it was all over.

He was going to lose her, and that hurt. He cared about Emma. Not as a protector, but from somewhere deep inside, and he hated it. Because to her he was just somewhere to run.

"I didn't mean it like that," she said in a rush.

"Sure you did." His smile was cold and his eyes hot.

"You meant it exactly like that. And you're right. My job is to stand between you and the bad guys and catch the bullets."

"Maybe at first, but it's not like that anymore. I—"

"I don't want to hear it, and I don't have time to argue with you."

"Gabe—"

He cut her off again. "If the killer is a deputy marshal, he has access to everything. He's looking at everything, picking apart every detail. He'll figure the fax out eventually. Patrick's dead and you're missing." His voice got louder with every word. "That damned fax might as well be a map of Washington with a great big arrow pointing here!"

"I didn't send it!" she yelled back. "You did!"

The accusation hung in the air between them.

"Go away, Emma," he said when he had control of himself again. "Just get the hell away from me for a while and let me think. I've got a lot to do before tomorrow."

"Tomorrow?"

"We're leaving." He didn't make any attempt to break the news to her gently. He didn't care anymore. "We'd leave now, but it would cause too much talk if the bar were closed tonight. They'd start looking for us. If we leave tomorrow morning, we'll be gone a good twelve hours before anyone knows we've left."

"We? You'd go with me?"

"Until you're safe. And let's get one thing straight. I owe Patrick, not you."

Emily didn't argue; she couldn't. There wasn't much fight left inside her. Intending to leave him alone so he could grieve for Patrick in private, she walked toward the stairs. But something made her pause before she went down. Over her shoulder she said, "Let's keep *everything* straight. I owe Patrick *and* you. Whether you like it or not."

She didn't expect a response, and she didn't wait for one. She just wanted to get away from Gabe as much he wanted her away. All the pressure of the past five days concentrated at the center of her chest, crushing the air out of her lungs. The world was closing in, taking away what little freedom she had.

Gabe was wrong about everyone having choices. She didn't. People didn't think when they ran. They just ran until someone stopped them or until they couldn't run anymore.

Right now she felt trapped in some violent chess game. Not a pawn, but a worthless queen who watched from her ivory tower while the real pawns—like Patrick—sacrificed themselves for her. They died, and she was responsible.

Telling Gabe should have erased some of the guilt she carried around, but it hadn't. The pain in his eyes— that one moment of denial before acceptance—had been almost more than she could stand. Then there were all the questions he didn't ask—ones that would have hurt too much to answer. Eventually he'd ask about Patrick's last words. And she'd have to relive it.

Emily wandered through the quiet bar, wanting to scream, wanting to push out all the anger and fear and hurt that had accumulated inside her. It was too much to carry around. Way too much. Her hands curled into fists as she realized that what she really wanted to do was have Gabe put his arms around her and tell her that everything would be okay. She wanted his strength so badly, she ached.

Knowing she had to do something to release the tension, she decided to take a walk. She couldn't stand the waiting anymore. Yeah, a walk would be good, she told herself. Right now it didn't matter that a walk was dangerous, that somebody might be out there. Anything would be better than waiting. Somehow she couldn't manage to care that someone wanted to kill her. Nothing could be worse than the betrayal she saw in Gabe's eyes, or the guilt in her own heart for leaving Patrick.

Emily grabbed Gabe's coat, which was thrown over the bar, and then she saw the skates. The decision was easy. Really no decision at all. There would be no one to watch her, no one to judge her. There would be only the ice and Emily Quinn.

Ice was the one thing in her life she could control.

Gabe leaned against the pool table for a long time after Emma went downstairs. Finally he picked up the eight ball, rubbing his thumb over the surface. With a smooth motion he put some spin on it and sent it gliding across the green felt. The ball curved as though guided by a targeting computer and slid gracefully into the far corner pocket.

"We were pretty good at pool, buddy." Patrick wasn't in the room, but it didn't matter. "And gin. We were good at that game, too, as I recall. Good at both of 'em." Gabe smiled. "Until we tried *drinking* gin and playing pool. That combination didn't work out too well."

Gabe frowned. Emma didn't work out too well either. She'd already gotten Patrick killed and was doing her level best to destroy him or at least the part he guarded most carefully—his heart. Angrily he sent another ball spinning into a pocket.

When had she stolen past his defenses? What was it about her that made him want what he couldn't have? Why her and not the other women he'd known? Even now, despite the anger and loss, he felt a need to grab hold of her, as if holding her would make some of the pain at Patrick's death go away. When his arms were around her, Emma created an anchor for his soul.

And he hated that.

As much as he needed to blame her for his vulnerability, Emma wasn't responsible, not entirely. The six-year-old boy inside him deserved most of the credit. That boy had spent his life trying to earn love with one outrageous deed after another.

He'd gotten attached to Emma because old habits were hard to break. She had needed him; he volunteered to be the hero. The reality was you couldn't make someone love you. You couldn't control love. You weren't loved because you were worthy.

Thank God, he realized that before he made the mistake of falling all the way in love with her. If he kept his distance, he'd be fine. Unfortunately, keeping his distance required controlling his emotions. How could he do that, when the anger was still there, right on the surface?

Beneath the anger was another layer of emotion, one

that was also hot and intense. And just as dangerous. No, the second emotion was *more* dangerous. Anger he could control. Passion had no master.

Wart rubbed against his leg, offering support. Gabe hunkered down and let his fingers sink into the cat's fur. "What the hell are we going to do?" Wart purred loudly. "Yeah, I know. Do the job. Stop wanting. Stop feeling. I know the drill. I just don't know if I can do it this time."

The bar was empty when he walked down. He called her name, surprised that she wasn't visible. When she didn't answer, he quickly checked the back and the rest room. Coming up empty forced a curse from him. And so did the fact that his coat was gone.

No, he told himself, refusing to consider the obvious. She didn't take off. She didn't run. She wasn't that stupid.

But she was that scared. Scared people did stupid things all the time. Add to the fear the fact that they'd both been hurt and angry and ready to explode.

Then Gabe noticed the skates were gone too.

"You wouldn't," he whispered. But he knew she had. Marsha Jean had planted that seed well. The pond was an easy walk. A couple of miles. Deserted, shielded from the road by trees.

Gabe hit the door at a dead run, not bothering to grab another coat. He didn't plan to be gone long, just long enough to throw Emma into the truck and drag her back to where he could protect her. Despite his whispered encouragement, the engine decided to play hard to get all of a sudden. On the fourth crank and the first threat, it finally roared to life. Gabe kicked it into reverse and engaged the heater, cursing Emma with every breath.

He didn't know how long she'd been gone. Anything could happen. The damned ice on the lake could crack. That ankle could give out; she could fall. A trip to the hospital would be disastrous at this point. The worst-case scenario was that they'd been found already. That someone had been watching, waiting for an opportunity to dispose of her quietly and without witnesses.

That possibility was too real. Gabe refused to consider it. It didn't matter anyway. When he got his hands on her he was going to kill her. Or do something else equally foolish.

The truck flew down the road, skidding as he hit the brakes to make the sharp turnoff for the pond. It was a couple of hundred yards back from the road. The place was as deserted as Marsha Jean promised. Not a vehicle or a house in sight. Twenty or thirty trees dotted the bank around a small amoeba-shaped pond. An indistinct path wound its way down the slope into the trees.

Gabe shut off the engine and scanned the area, finding what he looked for almost immediately. Emma sat on a fallen log at the edge of the pond. She'd already shed his coat and was lacing up the skates, oblivious of his arrival. And just as oblivious of anyone else's approach. Relief suddenly took a backseat to anger. How did the woman expect to stay alive if she kept making herself a target?

Grimly Gabe slipped out of the truck, about to yell. As soon as she took the ice, his words evaporated under the weight of her need. Every ounce of concentration she had was centered downward. She had ignored her own safety and slogged two miles in snow to get to this pond. Gabe didn't know what the ice could give her, but he knew he couldn't stop her. Not yet.

He checked the road a second time, and then reached for the blanket beneath the seat. He wrapped it around his shoulders and waited for his first real glimpse of Emily Quinn. Shaking his head, he realized she was more cautious on the ice than off. She inspected every inch of the surface—despite Marsha Jean's assurances that it was rock solid.

Once she was comfortable, she adjusted to the feel of the ice quickly, executing showy little turns and skating backward. Gabe kept one eye on the road and one on her. He knew the faded black stretch pants covered the pair of longjohns he'd lent her that morning. His yellow sweater was layered over a couple of T-shirts for warmth. She had on his gloves, and he found that small intimacy sexier than he could explain.

God, she was graceful, he thought as he watched her. Every movement perfected by a lifetime of practice. Even in hand-me-down clothes and borrowed skates she etched poetry into the ice. Several times she performed bits of complicated, obviously choreographed routines, gathering speed, and building up to something. But then she'd just stop. Unexpectedly sad for her, Gabe realized she couldn't finish the routines because she couldn't jump. He wondered what she'd been like before the accident.

As he watched her pick up speed again, he tried to remember which ankle she'd injured, but he couldn't tell. Even when she attempted the impossible. Stunned, Gabe watched Emma launch herself into the air. The whole stunt was over before he had time to rush down to the ice and pick up the pieces when she fell.

But she didn't fall after the jump. She didn't stumble. She didn't even miss a beat. A second later she completed another jump. This time she hung effortlessly in the air, her body rotating twice. When she landed without a wobble, he understood why sports writers assumed the gold medal was hers for the taking.

Gabe tried to make sense out of the unbelievable. Emma shouldn't have been able to jump at all with a bad ankle. *"I can't feel the ice."* Her exact words.

The first jump, the one that looked simple, might have been explained as her need to try something easy, just to see if she could do it. But he didn't have to be a skating expert to know that the second jump was beyond the average skater's ability. And he didn't like the implication.

Gabe closed his eyes against the truth. Not that it did any good. The truth simply rerouted itself and formed a knot of uncertainty in his gut. If there wasn't anything wrong with Emma's ankle, then she'd used the injury as an excuse to walk away from the dream she said was never hers. How many more dreams would she walk away from before she found one she cared enough to fight for?

You don't know for sure that she walked away from this one.

A bitter sigh slipped out. No, he didn't know for certain. But if she did, Emma was running from more than a gunman. She was running from a past she didn't like to a future that had no name, certainly not his.

If he needed any more proof that she was using him,

he'd found it. The lady was a world-class liar. Literally. She'd fooled the whole world. Fooling one retired SEAL must have been a piece of cake for her. The vulnerable act. The tears. She was good. Real good. And smart enough to know that he'd try harder to save her if he fell in love with her.

Well, he was through being used.

He walked down to the pond while she stroked leisurely across the ice, occasionally tossing in fancy footwork. When he reached the bank, he traded the blanket for his coat and waited for Emma to see him. If a person could stutter on skates, that's what she did. For several moments he thought she might turn and stroke the other way. She didn't; she squared her shoulders.

As she got closer, he could see her cheeks were red and so was the tip of her nose. Everything about her seemed more alive. That vitality simultaneously knocked his heart into next week and infuriated him. The contrast was too painful.

"How does it feel to be alive when Patrick is dead?"

TWELVE

In one staggering instant all the peace Emily had found on the ice faded.

Anger she expected—because she'd left without even a note. Hate she could have understood—because Patrick's death was a secret she shouldn't have kept. But his cruelty was intolerable. No matter how much pain he was in or how much he wanted to fight, he didn't have the right to inflict this kind of guilt. She did a fine job of that all by herself.

She backed away, trying not to give him the confrontation he so desperately wanted. "Don't do this."

"Don't do what? Don't protect you?" Gabe reached out and snagged her arm before she went too far. He hauled her up onto the bank, fingers digging into tender flesh. "Don't point out that you make a really easy target for someone who wants to kill you?"

"This isn't about protecting me," she told him coldly.

"It sure as hell is, baby." The intensity was back in

his eyes, and so was the heat it generated within her. "Because if I don't keep you safe, Patrick will have died for nothing. Or doesn't that matter to you?"

For a few moments they stood, gazes locked. She waited for an apology that never came. Finally, she pried his fingers loose and pushed past him to undo the skates.

"I can't even believe you have to ask." Emily sat down and attacked her laces with all the anger she refused to let show in her voice. "You weren't there, Gabe. I was. I'd give anything in the world to change what happened that night. But I can't. And neither can you."

Her hands were shaking by the time she finished. Gabe said nothing, watching her like a biased judge with his mind made up. She refused to care about his reaction. Skates off and shoes on, she stood up. She didn't falter as she faced him.

"I'm sorry if I worried you. I'm sorry for being stupid. I'm sorry for needing your help. I'm sorry for lying to you. And if you can't forgive me, then fine—I'll be sorry for that too. But don't you ever ask me if I care about Patrick. I know exactly why he died. I have to carry that inside me every day. I don't need to hear it from you too."

"Of course not. You've already gotten what you need from me, haven't you?"

"How could I have?" she scoffed. "There's not a compassionate bone in your body. Why is that, Gabe? Are you afraid you might slip up and feel something real? Something you can't control? Now, wouldn't that be a cryin' shame?"

She slung the skates over her shoulder and headed for the truck. When they were halfway home, it occurred to her to wonder how long Gabe had watched her skate.

After the fiasco at the pond, conversation had become a mine field of emotions. Gabe made plans, and Emily agreed to them. Other than that she stayed out of his way.

What else could she do? Fate conspired so that she had very little choice. It was snowing and cold. She had no car, no money, and if she were honest, no desire to leave Gabe's protection. He was a hard man who dealt in hard solutions. Right now she needed hard solutions in her life.

Complicating everything was the sensual current that flowed between them. It wouldn't go away—despite the danger, despite the unresolved issues between them. Maybe it was Patrick playing one last cosmic practical joke on Gabe. Maybe it was simply that the energy made them feel alive. Whatever the reason, they got to each other in a way that defied common sense. The awkward silences only made the strain worse.

Gabe had finally gone down to the bar early and taken the tension with him. Unfortunately, the reprieve was over, and now it was time for the ex–Mrs. Gabriel to take another stab at fooling all of the people all of the time. Including Gabe.

Emily stared at the bathroom mirror and decided that "Emma" was the only positive element in this whole disaster. It was past time for her to start redefining herself, because Emily Quinn had never existed except in her parents' imaginations.

The former ice princess certainly wouldn't have been caught dead in this low-rent blue-jean miniskirt and cowboy boots. Or in the little white "muscle T" she wore beneath an oversize cotton sweater. It might have been a rich forest green at one time, but it was faded now.

The neckline kept slipping as she walked down the steps to the bar. Emily stopped and fussed with it to give herself an excuse to avoid Gabe a little bit longer. The limits of their relationship would change when she entered the bar. As Emma Gabriel it was her job to tease Gabe, to act like the ex-wife leading him on a merry chase. Walking out there would be like taking the first drink out of a potent bottle of scotch.

She took a deep breath and opened the door.

The angle was different, but the situation felt like a replay of that first night. She was still looking for a man, but this time she knew it was Gabe. And she knew he wanted her out of his bar and out of his life as quickly as possible.

He had one hand on his hip, the other planted on the bar. Behind him were the rows of liquor bottles and the antique cash register. For a second Emily found herself wishing that she'd told him everything immediately.

Hindsight was always so cuttingly precise. And worthless.

The Monday-night crowd was even bigger than the Saturday-night crowd. Emily wove her way through the chairs, trying not to let the incredible number of strangers make her anxious. Her hands were already fisted at her sides before she found a familiar face. She forced herself to smile at Angus Deady. He nodded, but he seemed to have transferred his interest to Marsha Jean. The waitress's T-shirt sported a Medic Alert emblem and instructions IF UNCONSCIOUS, ADMINISTER CHOCOLATE.

Slipping behind the bar, Emily whispered, "It's snowing. Why are they all here?"

"You're good for business, Emma." Gabe ran his eyes over her, taking in the fact that she had appropriated his favorite cotton sweater. He didn't object, since it hid a great deal he wanted hidden tonight. He'd let himself get distracted the night before, let someone slip by him. That wasn't going to happen tonight. Or ever again. "They've come to see the woman who divorced me."

Stunned, she cast a glance over the room again. The crowd was mostly men, but there were a lot of women. She had overlooked them the first time, because women weren't a threat. Now she wasn't so sure.

The ladies might not be carrying weapons, but none of them looked particularly pleased with her. Emily almost laughed. The ice princess might not be the news *du jour* in this town, but Emma Gabriel sure was.

Well, since everyone was so interested in her relationship with Gabe, she'd give them a hint. Wasn't that her job? To convince them that Gabe and Emma were an item? She turned back to the man and tiptoed her fingers provocatively up his chest.

"I hope I'm not cramping your style, dear," she said in her best blond-sexpot-ex-wife voice.

Gabe caught her wrist, not because he minded the message she sent to the other women, but because he'd spent all day trying to deal with his feelings for her, trying to shove them into a dark corner, where they could be forgotten. Her touch brought everything rushing back. "Put your claws back in, *sweet cheeks*. I've been faithful to the memory of what we had."

"We didn't have that much," she shot back, irritated that he'd removed her hand. There was nothing like playing to a full house, and the guys at the bar were straining to hear. "Just those two nights in Vegas, and that was so long ago. And of course that first night you couldn't— Well, you know."

Several of the guys choked on their drinks, spewing liquor onto the bar. Gabe clenched his jaw, and when he relaxed she knew she was in trouble. Her first clue was the wicked smile on his face.

"No, I couldn't," he said regretfully, "but you've lost a lot of weight since then. I believe I could carry you across the threshold now."

Emily managed to hold on to her gasp, barely. He was good, but not good enough. Okay, the gloves were off. Before the night was over, Gabe was going to crawl. Under control once more, she flapped the front of her sweater, making sure Gabe got a good glimpse down the front of it. Shouldn't be a problem considering his height.

"Is it hot in here?" she asked as Marsha Jean came up with a drink order, but answered her own question. "It is hot in here. This sweater has to go."

"No!" The word was a command from Gabe.

"Ah, look at that—a lovers' spat," Marsha Jean commented. "How sweet."

Gabe ignored her jibe, but lowered his voice as he

uncapped two beers. "You take that sweater off, and I'm locking you upstairs. You understand?"

"Honey," Marsha Jean said as she took the bottles, "we don't need a bar fight tonight."

"What makes you think there'd be a fight?" Emma asked.

Marsha Jean laughed. "You mean besides the fact that just looking at you is punishable by death? The bartender here being the executioner, of course."

Gabe glared at his waitress. When she retreated, he turned his attention to Emma. "About three seconds after the men in here see that flimsy red bra of yours showing through that white T-shirt, all hell's going to break loose."

"No problem, then," Emily told him maliciously, and crooked her finger to bring him closer. Whispering, she explained, "Because I'm not wearing a bra."

She followed Marsha Jean to an empty table that needed busing.

"Emma Gabriel, you are *bad*," Marsha Jean told her as she plucked a glass from the table and wiped off the circle of water. "But you better be careful. I've never seen Gabe like this. There's something hot and dark inside that man. I'm not so sure you should be stirrin' him up right now."

"Too late."

Emily put the tray down and planted her palms firmly on the table as if she were declaring war. Looking back over her shoulder, she caught Gabe staring at her backside, especially where the little slit threatened to expose too much. She turned back to the waitress. "As you would say, I've done put my spoon in the wrong pan."

"Well, could you at least stop stirring long enough to give me some help out here?" She lowered her voice. "Everybody wants details. I deserve a medal or something for keeping this quiet. I've been cool. I've been clever, but all this on-the-spot prevaricating is slowing me down at every table. It flat out takes too long. I figure they'll be too polite to ask you."

"I wouldn't bet on it," Emily said softly, and decided that Marsha Jean deserved more than a Purple Heart. Not many people could be trusted to keep a secret this juicy. Most people would have accidentally on purpose dropped little hints here and there. But not Marsha Jean. Emily wondered how many men bothered to look past her flamboyant exterior to the kind, generous woman inside.

"If they're insensitive enough to ask you questions," Marsha Jean told her, "spill a drink in their lap. That's what I do."

"Got any other tricks and tips?" Emily asked.

"None that God doesn't include in every woman's option package."

The rest of the evening Emily, aka Emma, walked a fine line. Every offhanded comment, every lie, had to match the one she told before. Each time she delivered a drink, she judged the man against a fuzzy memory. Every time someone walked in, her heart pounded a little until she was sure.

By closing time she had ruled out everyone, even the guy in the back who refused to look up. She'd also acquired an apron that was more like a wide white pocket, a good ear for drink orders, and Gabe's attention.

"Last call!" Gabe shouted for the benefit of the few remaining customers. It was a quarter to midnight. The crowd had begun to thin early, mostly because the snow had picked up steadily.

"So soon?" Emily asked facetiously as she climbed up on a stool. "What if I haven't made up my mind who I want?"

As if he hadn't heard her outrageous question, Gabe gave a White Russian a lazy stir and handed it off to Marsha Jean, who was clearly torn between staying to hear his reaction or collecting a tip. The tip won. When he was alone with Emma, he kept his voice low, just loud enough that she could hear.

"Darlin', you know who you want. You've made that real clear all night. You just don't know *what* you want. So I'll help you out. What you want"—he leaned a forearm on the bar and then casually traced the white strap that showed at the edge of her sweater—"is me inside you. Consider this a warning, Emma, you got my attention. I don't have to like you to want you. And if you keep playing this game, I'm going to do something about it."

"I'm playing the part you assigned me," she reminded him in a whisper. She couldn't pull back because he still had a finger in the neckline of her sweater.

"You're playing at being a bad girl. But that's okay. I like bad girls. They take what they want because it makes 'em feel alive."

He straightened up, satisfied with the effect of his words. Her breathing had quickened and her green eyes were wide. Leaning back against the cash register, he crossed his arms. "I'll tell you one more thing. I also like good girls who play at being bad. 'Cause when they're bad, it's just for me."

For Emily it was as though Gabe opened up her soul and dragged out another dirty secret. Her whole life had been spent in the spotlight—squeaky-clean Emily Quinn, who never kissed on the first date and who lost her virginity on the pristine sheets of a bed in a Canadian hotel and never broke a sweat. Sex didn't scare her. But making love to Gabe did. She couldn't imagine holding anything back.

Because of him, the bad girl she'd kept hidden for so long wanted to come out and play.

"I've got to help Marsha Jean." She scrambled off the stool, not caring how transparent her excuse was. Unfortunately, Marsha Jean had absolutely everything under control.

Unwilling to go back to the bar and face Gabe, Emily fished in her apron for a quarter and surveyed the jukebox selections. Not a single soul had come close to recognizing her tonight, and the guy that scared her last night hadn't come back. Both those accomplishments should be worth celebrating with a song. Surely Gabe had something appropriate on this thing.

While Gabe shooed the last of the stragglers and Marsha Jean out, Emily tried to focus on the list of titles, but her brain was too preoccupied to make much sense of the words. They finally blurred as she heard the door close and the locks snap into place. Emily's heart thudded sickeningly in her chest. One by one the lights went out. The only illumination left was the glow of the jukebox and whatever light filtered through the small, high windows from the floodlights outside.

She was alone with Gabe, and they both knew what was about to happen.

The sound of her quarter clinked loudly as it hit the coin bin. Blindly she pushed a couple of numbers. Anything was better than the silence. A second later, Patsy Cline began to sing *Crazy*.

Horrified, Emily realized the song was perfect. She was certainly crazy for falling in love, and that's what she was afraid had happened. How could she have let herself fall for a man who would never allow himself to love her back?

Gabe crossed his arms and leaned against one of the support posts along the edge of the small dance floor, unwilling to let the moment slip away. They'd reached the point of no return a long time ago, and he couldn't shake the feeling that tonight would be all they'd have. All he'd have.

They'd been lucky, but it wouldn't last.

Since they'd been to the cemetery, he'd known why Emma was fighting the bond growing between them. She was afraid of letting someone get close enough to control her life again. He hadn't been looking to get emotionally attached to a woman who was going to leave. And he sure as hell hadn't been looking to fall in love with a woman who lied to him rather than trusted him.

Like you have a choice in the matter?

When Emma turned, the lyrics of the song had as much impact on him as the apprehension on her face. He saw something in her eyes that shouldn't have been there. Desire, but not passion, something else, something he recognized—a longing for what she couldn't have. That was an emotion he understood all too well.

Nervously, she put her hands behind her, holding on to the jukebox as she inspected the beat-up cowboy boots on her feet. "We had a good night."

"Not yet."

Emily's head snapped up. How could the man's voice tie her stomach in knots and stop her heart? She'd never felt like this before—not even the first time. All of her instincts told her that falling into bed with Gabe was meant to be. They were about to say something with their bodies that they couldn't or wouldn't say with words. Nothing would be the same afterward. If making love was a mistake, there would be no correcting it, no way to turn back the clock.

"Take off the sweater, Emma."

Heat flashed through her like lightning, restarting her heart and stopping her breathing. Slowly, not to tease him, but because her world had suddenly developed a glitch that made everything move in slow motion, Emily pulled the sweater over her head and tossed it into a chair. She ran her fingers through her hair to straighten it. Then she put her hands on her hips, fingers to the back and thumbs on her waist as she took a deep breath and forced herself to meet his gaze.

Desire was evident in the muscle that tensed in his jaw, in the half-closed eyes, and the way he shifted his feet as if his jeans were suddenly uncomfortable. Emily felt immeasurably better. She wasn't the only one on the hot seat.

Gabe allowed himself to enjoy the sight of Emma's

breasts as they strained the thin cotton, the tip of one nipple clearly visible in a shaft of light from outside; the other hidden by a shadow. Shoving away from the support, Gabe went to her, wondering how so much woman could be packed into such a small frame. She was all curves and softness, not a bone in sight.

Without a word he reached out to trace one of those curves, beginning with her shoulder and following the slope upward and around to her collarbone, down the center of her chest. As her breathing quickened, his fingers found the valley between the plump mounds that rose and fell in cadence each time she dragged in air. He let his thumb brush across the pebbled nipple as he tested the weight of her breast, lifting it, filling his hand.

Gabe silenced any second thoughts with his mouth, kissing her deeply. Soon her hands were as busy as his tongue. She found the buttons of his shirt and undid them, pulled his undershirt out of his jeans, and slid her hands over his belly, scraping his skin with her nails. When she unzipped his pants, Gabe dragged her hands away from danger.

"Upstairs," he said heavily.

"No."

That one husky word was enough to make his arousal throb and send need surging through him. Cupping her face, he couldn't resist kissing her before he murmured, "The bed is upstairs."

"I don't want soft." Her hands had found their way into his pants again, spreading the front and freeing him.

Caught between Emma's needs and his own, Gabe held on to the thread of sanity long enough to grab her arm and pull her into a dark corner, away from the door. She reached behind her and unfastened her skirt, giving her hips a little shimmy to encourage it to slide to the floor. Gabe swore and lifted her onto the booth table as she put her arms around his neck.

Gently he took her hands away and laid her back. He insinuated himself between her legs, but forced himself to wait, to enjoy the sight of Emma in those damnable red panties she fished out of the dryer every morning. All she had left of respectability was a little scrap of a T-shirt, a pair of cowboy boots, and red silk undies that were going to tear after the first good tug.

Emily watched as he shrugged out of his shirt, flinging it roughly behind him. There was nothing demure or elegant about the fire between them. She hooked the heel of her boot around his hip, silently asking for what she wanted. The pulse between her legs created an ache that could be satisfied only one way.

When he flung his T-shirt away too, she wet her lips. She could feel his heat through the wet silk of her panties, feel his hardness as he teased her, pulling her hips toward him, promising everything and yet delivering nothing except sweet torment. He pushed up her shirt, exposing her breasts to his hungry gaze. He cupped them and plucked at the sensitive nipples, finally bending over to taste them when she arched her back, offering herself.

He seemed to have all the patience in the world, making her grit her teeth against a moan, and then suddenly, as she wove her fingers into his hair and squirmed beneath his touch, she realized that Gabe wanted to force a moan from her. And he fought dirty. As the motion of his tongue and mouth pulled sensation after sensation through her, his hand moved between them, caressing her intimately, stroking the hidden nub and sending devastating little eddies of passion swirling outward. When he grabbed hold of her panties and ripped them off in one motion, she gave up, and the moan came out as his name, an urgent plea.

He sheathed himself and drove into her, forcing a ragged sigh of relief from her. Each time he withdrew she found herself trying to hold on, trying to keep him inside. It was her turn to force a groan from him, to feel the tension as nature took control from both of them, setting the hard, fast rhythm that caught them both off guard and unleashed a shuddering climax that blazed through their souls and left them spent. Breathless.

Gabe recovered first, at least enough to know that he'd made a mistake pushing Emma to the edge of her sensuality. He'd caught himself in the trap. There had been no veneer of civilization between them. No meaningless endearments to hide behind. Just the stark reality that they were made for each other. Pieces of the same soul.

And for the first time Gabe admitted to himself that he had it backward. Maybe Emma didn't need him as much as he needed her. He wasn't sure he could let her go, but the hell of it was he didn't have a choice. She didn't belong to him. No one ever had. Not for long.

She was using him; he was just a port in the storm.

The pattern of being forgotten was a familiar one in his life. It had started long before he arrived at the orphanage. At eighteen he had joined the navy because he thought it was a chance to break the pattern. To have something real. But in the navy, just like in the orphanage, once the emergency was over, he had been forgotten until the next disaster, until he was needed.

Well, he was needed now. She was his now. He was overdue for a change of luck. Scooping Emma up, Gabe carried her upstairs and made love to her again. This time she chose the pool table. Neither of them asked for promises, and neither of them offered any.

Later, finally in bed, Emily lay in his arms, lazily nuzzling her face against his chest, wishing she could always feel this safe. That she could hide on a mountaintop with Gabe and not have to worry about the world or who she really was. When she was in his arms, she felt found instead of lost, real instead of make-believe.

"Dammit!" Gabe swore, and got up. "I left the bar coffee on. If I don't turn it off, the whole place will burn down. Hell, I'd better check everything again." He looked pointedly at her after he pulled on some jeans. "I was distracted."

They both jumped as the phone rang. Emily pulled on Gabe's shirt as he reached for it. "Hello? Marsha Jean! Why in hell are you calling this time of—"

Gabe's exasperation faded. His eyes caught and held Emily's as he asked, "What kind of questions?"

THIRTEEN

A prickle of fear touched the base of Emily's neck and slithered its way down her arms. She didn't know which she hated worse, the questions he asked or the silence as he listened to the answers.

"No!" Gabe said quickly into the phone. "You did the right thing. What was he doing at Lyon's? Did he leave when you did? How long ago was that?" He checked his watch. "Okay, then consider me warned. And as of now you're on paid vacation. I don't want you back at the bar until I call you. You just sit tight. . . . No. I don't want you around here, you understand? . . . And I am always careful."

When Gabe hung up the receiver, she could see his mind working, turning over the problem as he filled her in. "Some guy just scared the hell out of Marsha Jean. She stopped to pick up some milk at Lyon's In-'n-Out. The guy was in the back using the pay phone. He got off when she came in, almost as if he'd been waiting for her. Started talking to her and then asked questions about the bar and about you."

"And what's the bad news?" Emily joked weakly, feeling the panic began to stir in her stomach.

"She thinks she saw this guy in the bar last night, the night 'Emma' arrived."

Emily realized too late that she'd told Gabe everything except one last detail, so she confessed her final secret. "In the farmhouse . . . when I came down the stairs, I got confused for a minute. It was dark. I was already scared. There were two men, one standing over the other. Just for a second I thought the killer was Patrick."

At first she thought she was going to have to spell it out, but then she saw understanding dawn in his eyes, followed swiftly by fury. "The man who killed Patrick sat in *my* bar, drinking *my* liquor. I had him cold, and you let him walk away?"

"Gabe, I—I was confused. You talked me out of it! I thought maybe—"

"You thought wrong. If you'd told me about mistaking the killer for Patrick, we wouldn't be in this mess. If you'd told me about Patrick, we wouldn't be in this mess. If you'd shot the marshal when you had the chance, we wouldn't be in this mess. So do us both a favor, and stop thinking."

He took one step away from her and turned back suddenly. "Get dressed. We're leaving. Before the snow gets any worse."

Gabe issued the order as if she were a soldier and not the woman he'd made love with. Emily didn't argue, because "Gabe" was gone. The cold man giving orders was Archangel, and she didn't want to call down his wrath on her head any more than she already had. He was in no mood to listen to excuses or apologies. Besides, she was good at letting other people take control. It was what she did best, she thought bitterly. That, and keeping secrets.

While she dressed, Gabe checked his Beretta. The 9mm was the only gun he kept at the bar. Everything else was at the cabin. That would be their first stop. He needed more firepower. Patrick had tried it with one gun, and Patrick was dead.

He grabbed a couple of clips from the drawer by the bed and his coat. "Let's go."

"Where?" Emily asked as she followed him down the stairs and through the bar, figuring a request for information didn't come under the heading of argument.

"Away from here," came his curt reply.

The bar was dark, and Gabe left it that way. Before they'd crossed halfway to the door, the flicker of headlights raked the front of the bar, warming the bottom edge of the high windows. A split second later the lights winked out. Gabe halted and tilted his head, listening for something.

Emily held perfectly still, afraid to breathe and hoping her imagination was creating monsters where there were none. Then she heard it too—the sound of a car creeping into the parking lot. The tire chains chinked faintly as the car rolled over packed snow. But for Emily the most terrifying noise was the muffled creak of the cold metal as the car door was opened.

"Steady," Gabe whispered. He was already moving

her toward the back when they heard the first lock being jimmied open. A few more seconds and the guy would be in.

Despite the urgency, Gabe moved carefully through the stockroom to the rear door. His gut wanted to stay and take the guy out, but his brain knew his job was to avoid any confrontation until he could get Emma away. Until he could at least put a gun in her hand and give her a chance to protect herself. Now was not the time or the place.

He cracked the back door and waited to see if the guy had a partner. When no one came around the corner, he stepped out and pulled Emma with him. Snow was coming down with a vengeance. Gabe swore beneath his breath. They weren't going to get far in this.

"Let's go," he mouthed at Emma.

It wouldn't take the man long to discover they weren't upstairs asleep. They had maybe three minutes to get around to the front and gone before the shooting started. They paused again at the corner of the bar to check for a second man. The parking lot was empty.

"Now," Gabe whispered.

They sprinted for the truck. Gabe had to grab Emma as she tried to go around to the passenger side. The doors were locked, and he didn't have time to unlock them both. Cursing he fumbled with the key.

"Hurry," Emily whispered despite her promise to keep silent. Her fingers itched to snatch the keys away from him. She tried not to crowd him, but she couldn't help it. Her hand clung to his arm as she looked over his back to the bar. Any moment she expected Bookman or the marshal to come through that door and kill them.

The key slid smoothly in the second try, and Gabe shoved her inside. "Get in the truck and stay down on the floor."

A second later Gabe was inside. He pitched the Beretta on the seat and rammed the key home in the ignition. He didn't bother to shut the door or back up. He pushed in the clutch and let the truck roll backward before he started it. Then he shoved it in gear and hit the gas.

The sickening sound of fractured metal told him that he hadn't quite cleared the mailbox when he turned, but he didn't slow down until he was sure the heavy snow had obscured their tailgate. Gabe flipped on the headlights. "You can get up."

Slowly, Emily unfolded herself from her fetal position on the floorboard. Her hands were still shaky, and she was afraid to move the gun. Gabe noticed and moved it for her, placing it on the dash.

"Maybe it was Sawyer," she whispered as she leaned back against the seat. Her heart was still in her throat. "Maybe he graduated from rocks."

"No." Gabe thought about Marsha Jean and the questions. "It's not Sawyer."

"Let's go to the police," she said suddenly. "Maybe it's time."

"And tell them what? We think a U.S. deputy marshal is out there trying to kill us and that the marshal's office can't be trusted?"

"Willis would believe us."

"And what if he does?" Gabe shot back sharply. His attention was riveted to the road, which disappeared into an angry wall of white. Visibility was less than fifteen feet. "You'll be right back in the hands of the system that couldn't protect you to begin with. What kind of sense does that make?"

"But I've seen him now. I can identify him."

"Think, Emma. If they can bribe one agent, don't you think they can get to another one? Or two? Or however many it takes? They wouldn't let you testify against Bookman and they aren't going to let you testify against this marshal. He can burn them just as badly as Bookman could've."

"Then what are we going to do? We can't go to the police. We can't go to Marsha Jean's. And we can't drive in this storm. Not for long. The roads are probably closed."

"We're going to the cabin. That'll buy us some time."

The tone of his voice set warning sirens off in her head. "You mean enough time for the storm to be over so we can get out of here, right?"

"No. He won't wait that long, but we'll have enough time to prepare."

"Prepare for what? He can't follow us in this weather."

"It'll slow him down, but he'll come after us all the same. He has to. We're loose ends, and he's a tidy guy."

"He can't follow us in this weather!" Emily repeated. "No one could. How is he going to find the cabin?"

"Oh, he can find it. He screwed up with Patrick. This time he did his homework. I guarantee it. I bet he knew all about the cabin before he ever showed up in the bar. But he's still making mistakes. He figured Marsha Jean for dumb, and he picked the wrong night. The storm isn't going to do him any favors. He'll have to wait for it to let up, and by then I'll be ready."

"For what?" Emily asked, although she knew the answer. Gabe wanted revenge enough to turn them both into bait.

"I can take him at the cabin. It's my playground."

"What are the rules in this little game?"

"If I kill him, I win."

"And if he kills you?"

Gabe didn't answer, his eyes on the road and the worsening snow. Emily shivered, but it had nothing to do with the cold outside.

The cabin was about twenty minutes from town, off a logging road at the end of a long drive. Emily understood why he didn't call it home. Obviously, the place was built as a poor man's hunting retreat. Inside, there were two rooms—a living room with a wood stove, and a small room for supplies and gear. No kitchen. No bathroom. Only one window, one door. The springs in the couch were shot so badly that she could see the sagging middle in the dark.

"I bought it for the land," he explained. "Not the amenities. Sit down and stay out of my way."

"No problem. I'll just practice my sitting-duck imitation," she snapped, then wished she hadn't. The tension between them was thick enough without her foolishly adding to it. "Sorry. I snap when I'm terrified."

He didn't acknowledge her apology. Instead, he went straight to the small room and brought out a gas lantern. When he had it lit, he placed it by a tall metal cabinet that looked more like a bank safe than a storage cabinet. Emily caught her breath when he unlocked the doors.

"Souvenirs," Gabe said, anticipating her question. A variety of firearms was mounted on the inside walls. And obviously a few other toys he'd collected over the years. "All of it's legal. Most of it anyway. No explosives."

She watched as he took down another pistol like the one he had at the bar and slammed a clip in it. He laid it on a wooden TV tray along with some sort of radio gadgets and what looked like a spool of white thread. Finally he reached for a shotgun—*that* she could identify at least—and a box of shells.

As he opened the box, he told her, "I figure he won't be able to find the turnoff until the storm lets up. That should be about dawn. I'm going down to the front of the drive to put in an alarm system."

"Those radio things?" she guessed. "How?"

"Real simple." He started loading shells. "One of the radio things is a cheap sending device. Anybody with access to Radio Shack can whip one up. Works off a pin. The thread will connect from the device to a tree. When our boy drives in, the tires pull out the pin, and we get the signal on this little receiver. And then we throw a surprise party for him."

"How do you know he'll turn in the driveway?"

"He'll walk most of the way, but he'll want the car off the road. I would." Gabe pumped the shotgun, sending a round into the chamber. "Here." He held out the shotgun.

Recoiling, Emily shook her head. "No. It wouldn't

do any good. I couldn't actually hit anything I aimed at anyway."

"Then don't aim. Point it at a noise, shut your eyes, and pull the trigger. That'll be close enough." He motioned for her to take the gun again. "Lucky for you, in this world close enough counts in three things: horseshoes, atom bombs, and shotguns."

Slowly Emily took it, awkwardly laying it across her knees. The gun was heavy and alien to her.

"As soon as you shoot something, pump it again like I did." He scooped up the sending device and thread, slipping out into the snow without a backward glance. "Lock the door behind me."

He could have been gone an hour or five minutes. Either way, she was terrified every second, terrified he wouldn't come back. Terrified that if he did, she wouldn't know what to say or how to break through that icy wall he'd put up. She hated it.

Gabe hollered and came back in the door, she half rose to meet him, not that he noticed the smile of relief she couldn't keep off her face. He didn't acknowledge her in any way. Other than to tell her what to do, he hadn't looked at or spoken to her since Marsha Jean's call. He acted like a man doing a job for an employer he didn't even like. It was as if they'd never made love or as if he'd detached himself from his emotions.

Or she'd imagined them to begin with.

When he had checked the receiver and started a fire in the wood stove, Gabe finally shrugged off his coat and turned the lantern down. "First watch is yours. You take the chair. I'll take the couch. Wake me in an hour. Or if you hear anything. Anything at all."

"I don't have a wristwatch," she said as she got up to move.

He tossed her his. "Now you do. Dammit! Careful with that shotgun!"

Gabe hadn't meant to yell at her, but it was either that or pull her into his arms. She looked white as moonlight on snow. And scared. He was a bastard to ignore her, but he couldn't give in, wouldn't torture himself anymore.

Every time he gave in, something happened to remind him that there was nothing real between them. At least not for Emma. No trust. No love. Only the danger.

Forcing himself to settle in, he put one Beretta on the wooden tray within easy reach and one on the floor beside the couch. He turned his back to the door and closed his eyes. Sleeping anywhere, anytime, was a talent, but tonight it failed him. He couldn't remember the magic formula that turned off his brain and let his body rest.

Seconds turned into minutes before he finally began to relax. In the quiet, he imagined he could hear Emma's heartbeat along with his own. Then he imagined he heard her voice whispering to him.

"I know this is the wrong place, and God knows it's the wrong time, and you're asleep . . ."

Gabe's eyes snapped open at the tiny sniff that sounded so real, so muffled. She was crying as quietly as a woman could cry.

". . . but I'm scared to death that whoever's out there is going to kill you before you forgive me for Patrick. I keep seeing him, lying there, needing me. And I keep asking myself why I didn't stay. Why I didn't hold his hand and close his eyes. Gabe, I am so sorry I left him, but I couldn't . . . I couldn't do it. I couldn't pull that trigger. I tried. God knows I tried."

When he rolled over and sat up, Emma jumped so high she almost upset the shotgun, which was leaning against the wall. Her eyes were huge glittering circles of tears as she stood there, catching her breath. "I—I didn't mean to wake you."

"It's all right. You don't have to— It's all right. I understand."

"I never meant to hurt you," she promised, and licked a tear off her top lip. He'd never seen a woman who needed someone to hold her more than Emma needed him then.

He rested his forearms on his spread thighs and clasped his hands together. The only way he could keep his heart in one piece was to keep hands off her. Whatever she felt toward him was aroused by the need to feel alive, and not by love. It was a natural reaction. He didn't blame her, but he couldn't let it happen again.

"We called him Wile E., you know," he said, speaking of Patrick. "Wile E. Coyote. He was never very bright, but you couldn't kill the son of a bitch." His voice broke, and he realized that he never should have started this story. It was his turn to cry. "You could blow him up . . . drop him off a cliff . . . you could even shoot him. But you couldn't kill him. He was invincible."

"Gabe. . . ."

When she crossed the room and touched his arm, he was lost; he needed her as much as she needed him.

Right or wrong, he had one more chance to love her, and he took it. He told her he loved her with his mouth and his body, but not with words. That would have only made it more difficult to let her go when the danger was over.

She wasn't his, but when he came, he came inside her.

At the first gray light of dawn the alarm system did its job.

"Show time." Gabe turned off the receiver and cracked the door for a peek as he talked. "You take the shotgun and get into the supply room. Don't come out until I tell you to, and if anyone but me tries to open that door, shoot them. Pump the shotgun and shoot them again."

Gabe broke off to give her a hard look. "Are we clear on this?"

"No." Emily didn't like the plan. It was too much like Patrick's plan. She didn't think she could go through that again. "Why do you have to go out there? Why can't I go with you?"

"Because killing men is what I do," he said bluntly as he grabbed the Beretta and an extra clip off the tray. "And I do it a helluva lot better when I'm not distracted."

He opened the door wider and scanned the area. Satisfied, he slipped out into the cold. The black night was slowly giving up its hold on the sky, grudging every inch stolen by the dawn. A diffuse gray light washed the driveway, but purple shadows still clung to the woods.

As quietly as he could, Gabe faded into the woods on the left of the cabin. He moved from tree to tree in a smooth motion, always parallel to the drive, and his attention riveted on the trees across the way. If he were the marshal or the hit man, that's the approach he'd have chosen. More trees, better cover, better view of the cabin door and window. Finally he stopped about thirty yards from the cabin, setting his shoulder against the icy bark and bracing himself for the shot.

His hands stung as the cold seeped into them, but he didn't move them to his pockets to warm them. He couldn't take the chance. He might get only one shot at the man; he couldn't miss.

Gabe waited, motionless, constantly scanning the far side, searching for the movement that would give him his target. As the minutes passed, Gabe felt the hair on the back of his neck prickle. Slowly he turned toward the cabin, gut instinct telling him that too much time had gone by. Something was wrong.

Dammit! Whoever tripped that thread was playing with him or very, very good. Or both. Somehow he'd managed to slip by.

As swiftly as he could, Gabe silently retraced his steps. Pausing at the edge of the cabin clearing, he checked for footprints in the snow, trying to see if anyone had approached the cabin. From this angle all he could see were the indentations made by his own boots and the drifts of snow piled around the cabin and the woodpile.

He didn't like it. He didn't like it at all. Emma was alone.

Quickly Gabe checked behind him, giving the drive

and the area one last sweep. Then he searched the tree-line around the clearing. A few more minutes and dawn would be gone. For a second Gabe wondered if an animal had tripped the sending device, and then he saw the dark green fabric of a coat sleeve, just barely extending beyond the corner of the cabin. As if someone were waiting, arm upraised, leaning against the cabin and ready to shoot.

Gabe took an experimental step, gauging the sound of his footstep in the loose snow and the reaction of the coat sleeve. It didn't move. Gabe took another slow step, still close enough to the woodpile to dive for cover if the man heard him. Once Gabe made it to the side of the cabin, he forced himself to keep the same careful pace.

At the back corner of the cabin, Gabe waited and listened. Finally he risked a glance around the corner, and all he saw was the blue-black metal of a gun as it cold-cocked him. Stunned, Gabe staggered and felt his gun ripped from his hand. When his vision cleared, Gabe spread his hands and focused on the tall, familiar man who leveled a 9mm at his head.

"Archangel, I presume?" The man tossed away the Beretta. It landed beside the remains of the sending device. "Funny. I thought you'd be faster. And perhaps smarter."

"Obviously not."

"Obviously." He jerked his head toward the front of the cabin. "I believe I'll let you walk in that door first. In case you've planned any other surprises for me." He smiled. "You have, haven't you? Sure you have. You've lasted longer than Patrick. I'll give you that."

Gabe fought for control. No mistakes, he cautioned himself. No emotion. He had to be as cold as this bastard. It was their only chance. Slowly he turned and started for the front, his mind racing.

"Stop at the porch, Gabriel, and tell her we're coming in."

Gabe halted, his foot on the first step. "Emma! It's Gabe. We're coming in. Me first. Don't do anything stupid." Then he added, "Take my advice for once. You'll be safer that way."

"Nice touch," the gunman praised. "Let's hope she listens."

Gabe smiled grimly as he approached the door. "Let's hope."

He turned the handle and let the door swing open. Emma stood facing them, shotgun raised. And just as he told her, she pointed at the noise, closed her eyes, and pulled the trigger.

FOURTEEN

The moment Emma closed her eyes Gabe dove for the Beretta on the floor by the couch. He found the grip and rolled in the same motion. The force of the shotgun recoil knocked Emma backward; she went down hard, but Gabe's attention was focused on the silhouette in the doorway. When he fired, the man—already stunned by the damage Emma had done to his right arm—wavered like a cut tree right before it snapped and fell.

With a great deal of satisfaction Gabe softly called "Timber!" when the man hit his knees and pitched forward into the cabin. "That was for Patrick."

At his words the paralysis that gripped Emily evaporated. She realized she was still sitting on the floor, shotgun on her lap. As the man fell, she shoved the gun away. Hating the feel and smell of it.

Hearing her, Gabe tried to get up, but pain blindsided him and drove him back down. Nausea hit him in waves, and he knew he'd dislocated his shoulder in the dive. *Dammit*, he thought as his head rested against the floor. He was getting soft. He'd been out only a year, and he'd not only let someone get the jump on him, he'd forgotten how to dive and roll. At least the adrenaline had kicked in long enough for him to get the shot off. That was all that mattered.

"Gabe! Are you all right?" Emily tried struggling to her feet, not quite making it when she saw that Gabe was lying on the floor by the couch. She crawled over to him, chanting, "Please don't be dead. Please don't be dead. I need you. *Gabe!*"

"I'm fine." He held up a hand to reassure her as she reached him. "Just dizzy for a minute. I had to catch my breath."

"Oh, thank God! Don't you ever do that to me again!" she yelled at him.

Grabbing a handful of his shirt, Emily crumpled into a tearful heap at his hip, realizing she needed some oxygen, or she was going to pass out right alongside him. There was too much she wanted to say, so she sucked air in and out until her heart stopped racing and the faintness passed. Her hands were shaking so badly as she rubbed beneath her eyes, she could feel them vibrating on her face.

Emily spared a glance for the body in the doorway. She didn't look long because the weight of what she'd done bore down on her. She studied her hands, turning them over and over as if they could explain where the strength had come from. For so long she had thought of herself as weak, powerless to control her life.

In that split second before she pulled the trigger, something changed inside her. She knew what she wanted, and she knew what she had to do to keep it. "I didn't want your death on my conscience too. All I could think about was you, what you told me to do. That I didn't want you to die."

Gritting his teeth, Gabe knew where this was leading, and he had to stop her before she convinced herself that guilt and gratitude were love. Before he allowed himself to encourage her, to use her fear of being alone in the world as a way to chain her to him.

All his life he'd wanted to be important to someone, to be needed. Now he knew that simply being needed wasn't enough.

He wanted more for himself. More for Emma. He loved her enough to let her go. *Sister Mary Joseph's last lesson*.

Forcing himself up, he used his good hand to hold his arm tightly to his body. He ground out words through the pain. "You did what you had to do. We both did. Don't analyze it to death."

She twisted around at the strain in his voice. "Oh, my God, Gabe, you are hurt!"

"Don't," he told her, waving off her concern and her touch. "It's just a dislocated shoulder. I can manage."

Stung by the coldness in his tone, Emily slowly dropped her hands, wondering what she'd done wrong. She searched his face for a clue, but found only detachment, a stranger's face. There was no anger, no softness, no love, no emotion of any kind.

Uneasiness crept over her, tiptoeing into her soul and chewing up her certainty. She and Gabe had made some sort of commitment last night. Hadn't they?

Nothing was actually spoken, but it was implied. Wasn't it?

Suddenly she wasn't so sure anymore. Did she want him to love her so badly that she lied to herself to make it so?

Her mind raced as she tried to find something concrete to reassure herself. But there was nothing. No words of love, or of a future. No words at all. Just their bodies and passion in the night. Just two people trying to feel alive one more time before they died.

The truth closed in on her, and her heart began to ache. Her pride refused to let her cry. Backing away from him, she gave him the distance he wanted, emotionally and physically. "We need to get you to the hospital. If we wait, the shoulder joint will be too swollen for them to pop it in manually. They'll have to do surgery if that happens, and they have to X-ray it anyway. It could be broken, you know."

Emily knew she was babbling, but she had to do something to keep the awful blackness inside from swallowing more than just her heart. Without waiting for his response, she got their coats. Gabe was on his feet, his jaw clenched as she stretched up to put his coat around him without hurting his shoulder.

"Get the keys out of my pocket." While she did, he said, "Tell me you can drive a stick shift."

"Not great. Not for a long time, but I'll manage." She shrugged into her own coat, averting her eyes from the body on the floor. "What about—"

"Leave him. You go start the truck. I'll handle it."

"Handle what?"

"We need his keys in case his vehicle is blocking the

drive, and I need to check his pockets. If he's law enforcement, he'll have his badge. They don't go anywhere without it."

"You can't turn him over. Not with your shoulder. I—I'll do it."

"Emma, don't argue for once," he said wearily. "Just get the truck." When she held her ground, he said, "I don't want you to do this. All right?"

For a second he sounded like he cared, but then his voice hardened, eradicating the tiny flare of hope. She nodded. Even if he didn't care, he was right; she couldn't do it. There were too many bad memories waiting for her. So she slid by the body without looking.

Gabe was waiting for her by the time she'd finally figured out the gears. Before she could get out, he pulled open the passenger door. He didn't need her help getting in. That was obvious from the way he gritted his teeth and just did it. He was a Navy SEAL, by God! They could take a lickin' and keep on tickin', she thought bitterly, wishing her heart could perform the same trick.

"Cascade Valley in Arlington is the closest hospital." He gave her directions, swearing softly as she ground the gears.

"Sorry." Her second attempt was better.

When they passed the rent-a-car sedan, Gabe spoke again. "His name was Walker Nance. He carried a marshal's badge, and he had some transport and transfer papers on your hit man, Joseph Bookman."

"Well, now, that was a bright idea," she said sarcastically. "Sort of like letting the fox into the henhouse."

"Yeah, well, we don't know if he was doing the

transporting. Probably wasn't. The papers are probably proof that he dusted Bookman. And if Bookman's dead, your testimony no longer matters to the prosecutor. Or to whoever was paying Nance. You'll be free. You can have your life back."

Emily almost laughed. *Her life*—what a joke. That wasn't the life she wanted anymore, but she couldn't tell Gabe that. He didn't want to know; he probably wanted to pack her off as quickly as possible. His debt to Patrick had been paid in full. As far as he was concerned, canceled had been stamped across the account with a big rubber stamp.

"So, why risk it," she asked, picking up the conversation. "Why'd he come after me if he had already killed Bookman?"

"With you dead he could probably have continued as a deputy marshal, working both sides of the fence. And then there's the money. I'm sure he didn't get it all up front."

Tired from the effort of keeping his emotions off his face and out of his voice, Gabe turned away from her and stared out the window. The shadowy grays of dawn still hovered on the horizon, reminding him that he liked his world, as well as his choices, black and white. He liked simple. Loving Emma and letting her go was one of the grayest choices of his life.

He knew she was confused and hurt right now. He could see it in her eyes every time she glanced over at him, when she held open the emergency room door. She might bend, but she didn't buckle. Another couple of hours of being safe and she'd be thankful she hadn't done anything rash.

She'd get over it; the lady had guts. He had to give her that. Even under Chief Dayton's barrage of suspicious questions, she'd held it together.

Miles Dayton was in his early fifties, the kind of methodical individual who'd spent his whole life in small-town law enforcement, hauling in drunks and scaring the hell out of teenagers for speeding. Cases involving murder, corruption, ice skaters in disguise, and the Mafia didn't come up often. He wasn't at all sure they were telling the truth until Officer Willis walked in.

It took Willis all of half a minute to absorb what Gabe told him and to convince Dayton to have the King County sheriff's office run her name through the National Crime Information Computer.

King County called back in five minutes. They got a hit the instant they put in her name. Dayton mobilized the force. He sent Officer Willis out to the cabin, had the dispatcher call the King County coroner for a wagon, sent the part-time secretary out for muffins, and contacted the marshal's office in Los Angeles himself.

By early afternoon Dayton had "solved" the case of his career. Willis had placed a phone call to his friend in California. Deputy marshals from the Seattle office had come and gone, taking all the evidence and notes from their interviews. They'd also confirmed Bookman's death—one bullet, at the base of the skull. The marshal with him had been killed the same way.

"Well, I guess that about wraps it up, Miss Quinn," Dayton said. "They'll want to talk to you again, like they said, but they've got what they need for now. Just stay where they can find you."

Emily actually laughed at the irony of his advice. "That has not been a problem so far."

The police chief didn't see the humor. He gave her an odd look as she walked away, and turned to Gabe. "You'll see that she gets where she needs to go?"

"Yeah. I can handle that." Gabe followed her out, knowing that she planned to be on the 4:30 Community Transit bus.

Emily waited for him in the truck and drove him back to the Last Call. Sunlight glinted mercilessly off the fresh snow. Everything around her was bright and shiny and new. Except for her life, she thought as she pulled up. Fate had conspired to give her back the old worn-out one.

Nevertheless, she owed Gabe for saving her life. And more. She owed him a debt. He wasn't the only one who paid his bills.

If he didn't want her in his life, then she wouldn't force herself on him. She wouldn't beg. She wouldn't cry. She could even pretend her heart was in one healthy piece instead of broken all to hell. But whether he liked it or not, she'd find a way to pay him back.

Taking the keys out of the ignition when Emma made no attempt to do so, Gabe got out of the truck. "Careful of the glass by the door."

"Something else to add to the bill," she said under her breath as she climbed out.

"What?"

Emily winced. She hadn't meant him to hear, but since he had . . . Why not get it over with? She wasn't going to be here much longer anyway.

"I said, 'Something else to add to the bill.' One

more service, one more favor, kindness, whatever. I've been running a tab since I walked into your bar."

Unlocking the front door, Gabe said, "No."

"Oh, yeah, I have. I owe you *big*." She patted the black stretch pants, making herself smile brightly in case he bothered to look at her ever again. "I'm a little tapped out at the moment, but as soon as I get back to civilization, the new endorsement deals will go through." She closed the door behind her. "I still have the face if not the hair, and . . . um . . . well, I figure if I paid off the mortgage on the bar and the cabin that we'd be even."

Gabe felt his good hand curl into a fist of frustration. The only way they'd be even was if she loved him, and that wasn't going to happen in this lifetime. Not real love anyway. To her he was only a down-on-his-luck bartender. Well, he didn't take charity, and he sure as hell didn't want a reward for saving her life. All he wanted was for her to pack her bags and leave him alone to howl at the moon and break glasses against the wall.

Most of all, he wanted her to go before he said he loved her.

So he sighed like a man reluctantly forced to point out the obvious. Gabe met her gaze without flinching and said, "You don't owe me a thing. Whatever I did, I did for Patrick. Not for you. It's over. Do you get it now, Emily?"

He called her Emily, she realized. His words knocked the breath out of her just as surely as a fist to the stomach would have. *Emily*. That hurt her more than he would ever know. She could still hear his husky words in the dark: *Emily belongs to them. Emma is mine.* It was one of the memories she would have cherished, and now it was gone, tarnished.

"And, darlin', you'd better save your money, because as soon as those advertisers find out you faked your ankle injury, they're going to want all that money back. I don't think the Wheaties people will be too thrilled when they find out they have a coward on the box."

Finally Emily found her voice, her mind spinning as she realized he knew something no one else in the world did. "A coward?"

He dropped his shoulder and let his coat fall onto a chair. "I saw the jumps that day at Sutter's Pond. Damn! You were good. Even I could tell. You walked away from a gold medal, didn't you? Guess you found a way to show your parents who was in control after all."

Grabbing the closest chair, Emily sat down before she fell down. Gabe was pushing her buttons, pushing them hard. What for?

"Come on," he urged as he strode behind the bar. "You can tell me. We've been through a lot together. Need a drink? Well, I do. My shoulder is on fire."

Emily felt empty inside, parched, but a drink wasn't going to help. Wide-eyed, she stared at him, trying to make sense of it all, trying to pluck the one important detail out of the hundreds that spun in her brain. Only he wouldn't stop talking long enough for her to think clearly.

"If you want to repay me for all my trouble," he told her as he poured shots, "then leave me alone so I can get back to my life, and you can decide what you want to do with yours."

He brought a shot of whiskey to her table and set it down. "One for the road."

Shaking her head, she ignored him, couldn't let him distract her. Bits and pieces of the past few days were beginning to settle in her mind.

I was never much good with faith.

Control is just an illusion.

You can have your life back.

It's over.

You can decide what you want. . . .

Coward.

It's over.

It's over.

Those last two words kept repeating, pushing at her, nagging at her, throbbing in her consciousness until she finally got it. Stunned, Emily realized that Gabe, in his infinite wisdom, had decided that she needed to be sent out into the world to find what she wanted. He was trying to give her control of her life, trying to push her away so she wouldn't look back.

Just like Sister Mary Joseph did for him.

Only Gabe wasn't trying to protect Emily Quinn. He was trying to protect himself from rejection. To a man with Gabe's past, it was better to send her on her way than risk his heart. The abandoned six-year-old who'd never had anyone he could believe in was making his decisions right now.

Deliberately she reached out and picked up the shot glass. A little Dutch courage wouldn't hurt. She knocked the liquor back. It burned all the way down, warming her from the inside out. Or maybe the warmth came from the hope that Gabe might actually love her.

She had a chance if she was willing to fight for it. All she had to do was convince Gabe that she wouldn't change her mind and walk away, that she wouldn't wake up one day and reject him.

She sighed as she returned the shot glass to the table under his watchful gaze. He wasn't much good with faith. Maybe that's what she was supposed to teach him. If she was lucky, it'd take a lifetime.

"You found out a lot about me in a short period of time," she mused. "Wonder if I learned as much about you?"

"Does it really matter at this point?" Gabe said cuttingly.

"I don't know." She toyed with the edge of the glass. "Let's find out. You like your women to be women, and your emotions to behave. And when they don't, you banish them and put that I-don't-give-a-damn mask on. You're hell on a pool table, with or without a cue stick. No matter what you say, you love that damn cat and try so hard not to show it."

"Finished?"

"No. There's one other thing."

Gabe narrowed his eyes as Emma got up and took off her coat. She pushed her sleeves up and braced her feet. All the hurt and confusion were gone from her eyes, but not the vulnerability. Or the expectation. Both those emotions were there in full measure.

"You like being in control," she added to the list. "You like being able to say 'It's over.' But it's not over this time, Gabe. It's not over until *I* say it's over. You taught me that, and so did my dad, actually. But the point is, I'm not the same woman that walked into this bar three days ago. You can't make decisions for me. No one can but me."

"I haven't."

"Oh, yes, you have. You decided I don't know what I want. No," she corrected herself carefully, "you've decided I can't be trusted."

He picked up the shot glass and walked away.

"I heard this great joke the other day," she said, willing him to stop, willing him to listen. "A nun walks into a bar . . ."

That got his attention. He didn't turn around, but he stopped. *God, Emma, can't you just let me do the right thing for the right reasons for once in my life? Don't make me want what I can't have. Don't be grateful.*

A war of silence raged between them until he gave in, and asked, "What's the punch line?"

"She falls in love with a man who doesn't believe in love. And sometimes he pushes people away when he wants to pull them close. Because he's afraid they won't love him back. And the nun thinks maybe he just needs proof."

Slowly Gabe turned, afraid to believe what he heard offered in her voice. He searched her face, looking for signs of the shy, uncertain woman who walked into his life. He couldn't find anything but confidence and determination. The vise around his heart shifted and loosened a tiny bit, but he couldn't let go all the way. Not until he gave her one last chance to walk away, one last push.

He closed the distance between them. "You didn't

fall in love. You fell into danger. It's the situation, the gratitude, making you feel this way."

"I know the difference. And you know why? Because I'm *grateful* to Patrick." She broke her promise about crying then. She felt a tear roll down her cheek. "But I *love* you, Gabe. It's the only thing between me and an eternity of nothing."

Gabe felt her love wrap itself around his heart and seep into his soul, replacing the sadness. A weight lifted, and he realized that Patrick would always be with him. He sent Emma to love him. Forever.

"Sweet Emma, I have been waiting for you my entire life," Gabe said, wishing he had two good arms. He kissed her anyway. Long and hard. And afterward he rested his forehead against hers and said the words that lived inside his soul, words that would erase the painful silence he'd kept. "I love you, Emma. I have loved you for a very long time."

She kissed him again. As she broke the kiss, he could feel her lips curve into a satisfied smile. "How long? Exactly how long?"

The teasing tone in her voice warmed him, erasing the last of his doubts. "Darlin', I was lost the first time you looked at me."

Pulling back, she laughed. "I don't think so! I was wearing a nun's habit at the time!"

"Okay, so I'm not a saint."

"Good. Because I'm not looking for a saint."

"What are you looking for?" Gabe asked the question that he knew would be asked again and again over the years—a private joke between the two of them.

"I'm looking for you."

"I'm right here." Gabe drew her to him, resting his chin on her hair. "I always will be, Emma."

"I know." She buried her head against his chest, trying to be careful of his arm. "Would you really have let me walk out that door?"

Gabe smiled. "Not for long. And never again."

THE EDITOR'S CORNER

Warning: the LOVESWEPT novels coming next month contain large volumes of suspense, heavy doses of hilarity, and enormous amounts of romance. Our authors are professionals trained to provide stirring emotion and irresistible passion. Do try their fabulous novels at home.

A Loveswept favorite for many years and now a rising star in historical romance, Sandra Chastain delights us with a brand-new series, beginning with **MAC'S ANGELS: MIDNIGHT FANTASY**, LOVESWEPT #758. Just when quarterback Joe Armstrong has decided his life is over, the doorbell rings—and a long-legged enchantress makes him reconsider! Annie Calloway insists she isn't a vision or a witch, just someone who cares, but Joe doesn't want his soul saved . . . only a kiss that tastes of paradise. Weaving equal parts heartbreak and humor into a tale of sizzling sensuality and a little magic, bestselling author Sandra Chastain sends a heavenly heroine to the rescue of a wounded warrior who's given up hope.

If anyone knows just how delicious temptation can taste, it's Linda Cajio, who delivers a sparkling, romantic romp in **HOT AND BOTHERED,** LOVESWEPT #759. When he rises from the sea like a bronze god, Judith Collier holds her breath. She'd chosen the isolated Baja village as a perfect place to disappear, but instead finds herself face-to-face with a man whose gaze uncovers her secrets, whose caress brands her body and soul. Paul Murphy makes no promises, offers her only pleasure under a flaming sun, but how can the runaway heiress persuade a tough ex-cop they belong to each other forever? Let Linda Cajio show you in this playfully touching story of love on the run.

No one understands the tantalizing seduction of danger better than Donna Kauffman in **THE THREE MUSKETEERS: SURRENDER THE DARK,** LOVESWEPT #760. Rae Gannon fights back wrenching emotions when she recognizes the man who lay near death in the shadowy cave. Jarrett McCullough had almost destroyed her, had believed an impossible betrayal and shattered her life. But now the untamed mystery man is at her mercy, the air sizzling between them as raw need wars with furious despair. Donna Kauffman demonstrates just how erotic playing with fire can be in this white-hot beginning to her romantic suspense trilogy.

Linda Warren celebrates a love treasured all the more because it has been too long denied in **ON THE WILD SIDE,** LOVESWEPT #761. If she hadn't already tumbled to the track from her horse,

Megan Malone knew the sight of Bill North would have sent her flying! Eight years apart hadn't cooled the flames that sparked between the daredevil jockey and the handsome rebel who will always own her heart. Now, this brash rogue must convince a headstrong lady determined to make it on her own that two hearts are better than one. Praised for her evocative writing, Linda Warren raises the stakes of passion sky high in this wonderful romance.

Happy reading!

With warmest wishes,

Beth de Guzman

Shauna Summers

Beth de Guzman   Shauna Summers

Senior Editor   Associate Editor

P.S. Watch for these fabulous Bantam women's fiction titles coming in October. Following the success of her national bestseller THE LAST BACHELOR comes Betina Krahn's **THE PERFECT MISTRESS**: the story of an exquisite London courtesan determined to make a solid, respectable married life for herself and an openly libertine earl who intends to stay single and free from the hypocrisy of Victorian society; recognized for her sweeping novels of the

American frontier, Rosanne Bittner presents **CHASE THE SUN**: Captain Zack Myers joins the army for one purpose only—to take revenge on the Indians who'd destroyed his world, but Iris Gray longs for the power to tame Zack's hatred before it consumes their love—and even their lives; Loveswept star Peggy Webb now offers her most compelling love story yet: **FROM A DISTANCE** spans the globe from small-town Mississippi to the verdant jungles of Africa with the enthralling tale of one remarkable woman's struggle with passion and betrayal. Be sure to catch next month's LOVESWEPTs for a glimpse of these intoxicating novels. And immediately following this page, check out a preview of the extraordinary romances from Bantam that are *available now!*

Don't miss these extraordinary books
by your favorite Bantam authors

On sale in August:

LORD OF THE DRAGON
by Suzanne Robinson

MARIANA
by Susanna Kearsley

LORD OF THE DRAGON

by best-selling author
Suzanne Robinson

The day he was condemned and banished from England, his fellow knights thought they'd seen the last of Gray de Valence. But the ruthless, emerald-eyed warrior had done more than survive in a world of barbaric dangers, he'd triumphed. Now, eager to pay back his betrayers, de Valence has come home . . . only to find his plans threatened, not by another man, but by a volatile, unpredictable, ravishingly beautiful woman. Vowing her own brand of vengeance against the high-handed, impossibly handsome knight, Juliana Welles will do her best to thwart him, to tempt and taunt him . . . until all Gray sees—and all he wants—is her. Yet when a cunning enemy puts their lives in peril, the fearless knight will have to choose . . . between his perfect revenge and the passion of a lifetime.

Juliana threaded her way through the foot traffic on the west bridge—farmers bringing produce, huntsmen, reeves, bailiffs, women bringing dough to be baked in castle ovens. As so often happened, Juliana's temper improved with the distance between her and Wellesbrooke. Once off the bridge, she turned north along the track beside the Clare. She rode in this di-

rection through fields and then woods for over an
hour.

Juliana stopped for a moment beside a water-filled
hole in the middle of the track. It was as long as a
small cart. She remembered splashing through it
when she chased after her maid, Alice. A little way off
she could hear the stream churning on its way to join
the Clare. She would have to turn back soon, but she
was reluctant. She still hadn't found the jar containing
leaves of agrimony, a plant with spiky yellow flowers.
She needed the agrimony, for one of the daughters of
a villein at Vyne Hill had a persistent cough.

Clutching her cloakful of pots, Juliana searched
the woods to either side of the track for the small
white jar. All at once she saw it lying on the opposite
side of the path at the base of a stone the size of an
anvil. So great was her relief that she lunged across
the track. She sailed over the puddle of water, but
landed in mud. Her boots sank to her ankles.

"Hell's demons."

Stepping out of the ooze, she picked up the jar,
balanced on the edge of the mud and bent her knees
in preparation for a jump. At the last moment she
heard what she would have noticed had she been less
intent on retrieving the jar. Hoofbeats thundered
toward her. Teetering on the edge of the mud, she
glanced in the direction of the stream. Around a bend
in the track hurtled a monstrous giant destrier, pure
black and snorting, with a man astride it so tall that he
nearly matched the size of his mount. Juliana stumbled back. She glimpsed shining chain mail, emerald
silk and a curtain of silver hair before a wall of black
horseflesh barrelled past her. An armored leg caught
her shoulder. She spun around, thrown off balance by
the force of the horse's motion. Her arms flew out.

Pots sailed in all directions. Legs working, she stumbled into mud and fell backward into the puddle. As she landed she could hear a lurid curse.

She gasped as she hit the cold water. Her hands hit the ground and sent a shower of mud onto her head and shoulders. Juliana sputtered and wheezed, then blinked her muddy lashes as she beheld the strange knight. He'd pulled up his destrier, and the beast had objected. The stallion rose on his hind legs and clawed the air, snorting and jerking at the bridle. Those great front hooves came down and landed not five paces from Juliana. More mud and dirty water spewed from beneath them and into her face.

This time she didn't just gasp; she screamed with fury. To her mortification, she heard a low, rough laugh. She had closed her eyes, but now she opened them and beheld her tormentor. The knight sat astride his furious war horse as easily as if it were a palfrey. He tossed back long locks the color of silver and pearls as he smiled down at her, and Juliana felt as if she wanted to arch her back and spit.

Juliana scowled into a gaze of green that rivaled the emerald of the length of samite that draped across his shoulders and disappeared into the folds of his black cloak. It was a gaze that exuded sensuality and explicit knowledge. Even through her anger she was startled at the face. It was the face of the legendary Arthur, or some young Viking warrior brought back to life—wide at the jaw line, hollow cheeked and with a bold, straight nose. The face of a barbarian warrior king, and it was laughing at her.

"By my soul," he said in a voice that was half seductive growl, half chuckle. "Why didn't you stand aside? Have you no sense? No, I suppose not, or you wouldn't be sitting in a mud puddle like a little black duck."

Shivering with humiliation as well as the cold, Juliana felt herself nearly burst with rage. The knave was laughing again! Her hands curled into fists, and she felt them squeeze mud. Her eyes narrowed as she beheld the embodiment of armored male insolence. Suddenly she lunged to her feet, brought her hands together, gathering the mud, and hurled it at that pretty, smirking face. The gob of mud hit him in the chest and splattered over his face and hair. It was his turn to gasp and grimace. Teeth chattering, Juliana gave him a sylph's smile.

"And so should all ungentle knights be served, Sir Mud Face."

She laughed, but her merriment vanished when she saw the change in him. He didn't swear or fume or rant in impotence like her father. His smile of sensual corruption vanished, and his features chilled with the ice of ruthlessness and an utter lack of mercy. In silence he swung down off his horse and stalked toward her. Juliana gaped at him for a moment, then grabbed her skirts—and ran.

MARIANA
by Susanna Kearsley

Winner of the Catherine Cookson Fiction Prize

The first time Julia Beckett saw Greywethers, she was only five, but she knew at once that it was "her house." Now, twenty-five years later, by some strange twist of fate, she has just become the new owner of a sixteenth-century Wiltshire farmhouse. But Julia soon begins to suspect that it is more than coincidence that has brought her here.

As if Greywethers were a portal between two worlds, she finds herself abruptly, repeatedly transported back in time. Stepping into seventeenth-century England, Julia becomes Mariana, a beautiful young woman struggling against danger and treachery, and battling a forbidden love for Richard de Mornay, handsome forebear of the present squire of Crofton Hall.

Each time Julia travels back, she becomes more enthralled with the past, falls ever deeper in love with Richard . . . until one day she realizes Mariana's life is threatening to eclipse her own . . . and that she must find a way to lay the past to rest or risk losing a chance for love in her own time.

I first saw the house in the summer of my fifth birthday. It was all the fault of a poet, and the fact that our weekend visit with a favorite elderly aunt in Exeter had put my father in a vaguely poetic mood. Faced with an unexpected fork in the road on our drive home to Oxford, he deliberately chose the left turning instead of the right. "The road less travelled by," he told us, in a benign and dreamy voice. And as the poet had promised, it did indeed make all the difference.

To begin with, we became lost. So hopelessly lost, in fact, that my mother had to put away the map. The clouds that rolled in to cover the sun seemed only an extension of my father's darkening mood, all poetry forgotten as he hunched grimly over the steering wheel. By lunchtime it was raining, quite heavily, and my mother had given sweets to my brother Tommy and me in a vain attempt to keep us from further irritating Daddy, whose notable temper was nearing breaking point.

The sweets were peppermint, striped pink and white like large marbles, and so effective at hindering speech that we had to take them out of our mouths altogether in order to talk to each other. By the time we reached the first cluster of village shops and houses, my face and hands were sticky with sugar, and the front of my new ruffled frock was a stained and wrinkled ruin.

I've never been entirely certain what it was that made my father stop the car where he did. I seem to remember a cat darting across the road in front of us, but that may simply have been the invention of an imaginative and overtired child. Whatever the reason, the car stopped, the engine stalled, and in the ensuing commotion I got my first watery glimpse of the house.

It was a rather ordinary old farmhouse, large and square and solid, set back some distance from the road with a few unkempt trees dotted around for privacy. Its darkly glistening slate roof sloped down at an alarming angle to meet the weathered grey stone walls, the drab monotony of color broken by twin red brick chimneys and an abundance of large, multipaned windows, their frames painted freshly white.

I was pressing my nose against the cold glass of the car window, straining to get a better look, when after a few particularly virulent oaths my father managed to coax the motor back to life. My mother, obviously relieved, turned round to check up on us.

"Julia, don't," she pleaded. "You'll leave smears on the windows."

"That's my house," I said, by way of explanation.

My brother Tommy pointed to a much larger and more stately home that was just coming into view. "Well, that's *my* house," he countered, triumphant. To the delight of my parents, we continued the game all the way home to Oxford, and the lonely grey house was forgotten.

I was not to see it again for seventeen years.

That summer, the summer that I turned twenty-two, is strong in my memory. I had just graduated from art school, and had landed what seemed like the perfect job with a small advertising firm in London. My brother Tom, three years older than myself, had recently come down from Oxford with a distinguished academic record, and promptly shocked the family by announcing his plans to enter the Anglican ministry. Ours was not a particularly religious family, but Tom jokingly maintained that, given his name, he had little choice in the matter. "Thomas Beckett! I ask you," he had teased my mother. "What else could you expect?"

To celebrate what we perceived to be our coming of age, Tom and I decided to take a short holiday on the south Devon coast, where we could temporarily forget about parents and responsibilities and take advantage of the uncommonly hot and sunny weather with which southern England was being blessed. We were not disappointed. We spent a blissful week lounging about on the beach at Torquay, and emerged relaxed, rejuvenated, and sunburned.

Tom, caught up on a rising swell of optimism, appointed me navigator for the trip back. He should have known better. While I'm not exactly bad with maps, I *am* rather easily distracted by the scenery. Inevitably, we found ourselves off the main road, toiling through what seemed like an endless procession of tiny, identical villages linked by a narrow road so overhung by trees it had the appearance of a tunnel.

After the seventh village, Tom shot me an accusing sideways look. We had both inherited our mother's Cornish coloring and finely-cut features, but while on me the combination of dark hair and eyes was more impish than exotic, on Tom it could look positively menacing when he chose.

"Where do you suppose we are?" he asked, with dangerous politeness.

I dutifully consulted the map. "Wiltshire, I expect," I told him brightly. "Somewhere in the middle."

"Well, that's certainly specific."

"Look," I suggested, as we appraoched village number eight, "why don't you stop being so pigheaded and ask directions at the next pub? Honestly, Tom, you're as bad as Dad—" The word ended in a sudden squeal.

This time, I didn't imagine it. A large ginger cat dashed right across the road, directly in front of our car. The brakes shrieked a protest as Tom put his foot to the floor, and then, right on cue, the motor died.

"Damn and blast!"

"Curates can't use language like that," I reminded my brother, and he grinned involuntarily.

"I'm getting it out of my system," was his excuse.

Laughing, I looked out the window and froze.

"I don't believe it."

"I know," my brother agreed. "Rotten luck."

I shook my head. "No, Tom, look—it's my house."

"What?"

"My grey house," I told him. "Don't you remember, that day the cat ran onto the road and Daddy stalled the car?"

"No."

"On the way back from Auntie Helen's," I elaborated. "Just after my fifth birthday. It was raining and Daddy took the wrong turning and a cat ran onto the road and he had to stop the car."

My brother looked at me in the same way a scientist must look at a curious new specimen, and shook his head. "No, I don't remember that."

"Well, it happened," I said stubbornly, "and the car stalled just here, and I saw that house."

"If you say so."

The car was running again, now, and Tom maneuvered it over to the side of the road so I could have a clearer view.

"What do you think it means?" I asked him.

"I think it means our family has bloody bad luck with cats in Wiltshire," Tom said. I chose to ignore him.

"I wonder how old it is."

Tom leaned closer. "Elizabethan, I should think. Possibly Jacobean. No later."

I'd forgotten that Tom had been keen on architecture at school. Besides, Tom always knew everything.

"I'd love to get a closer look." My voice was hopeful, but Tom merely sent me an indulgent glance before turning back onto the road that led into the village.

"I am not," he said, "going to peer into anyone's windows to satisfy your curiosity. Anyway, the drive is clearly marked 'Private'."

A short distance down the road we pulled into the car park of the Red Lion, a respectable half-timbered pub with an ancient thatched roof and tables arranged on a makeshift terrace to accommodate the noontime crowd. I stayed in the car, preparing to take my shift as driver, while Tom went into the pub to down a quick pint and get directions back to the main road.

I was so busy pondering how great the odds must be against being lost twice in the same spot, that I completely forgot to ask my brother to find out the name of the village we were in.

It would be another eight years before I found myself once again in Exbury, Wiltshire.

This time, the final time, it was early April, two months shy of my thirtieth birthday, and—for once—I was not lost. I still lived in London, in a tiny rented flat in Bloomsbury that I had become rooted to, in spite of an unexpectedly generous legacy left to me by my father's Aunt Helen, that same aunt we'd been visiting in Exeter all those years earlier. She'd only seen me twice, had Auntie Helen, so why she had chosen to leave me such an obscene amount of money remained a mystery. Perhaps it was because I was the only girl in a family known for its male progeny. Auntie Helen, according to my father, had been possessed of staunchly feminist views. "A room of your own," Tom had told me, in a decided tone. "That's what she's left you. Haven't you read Virginia Woolf?"

It was rather more than the price of a room, actually, but I hadn't the slightest idea what to do with it. Tom had stoutly refused my offer to share the inheritance, and my parents maintained they had no need of it, being comfortably well off themselves since my father's retirement from surgical practice. So that was that.

I had quite enough to occupy my time, as it was, having shifted careers from graphic design to illustration, a field I found both more interesting and more lucrative. By some stroke of luck I had been teamed early on with a wonderfully talented author, and our collaboration on a series of fantasy tales for children had earned me a respectable name for myself in the business, not to mention a steady living. I had just that week been commissioned to illustrate a sizeable new collection of legends and fairy tales from around the world, a project which excited me greatly and promised to keep me busily employed for the better part of a year. I was on top of the world.

Ordinarily, I'd have celebrated my good fortune with my family, but since my parents were halfway round the world on holiday and Tom was occupied with Easter services, I had settled for the next best thing and spent the weekend with friends in Bath. On the Monday morning, finding the traffic on the main road too busy for my taste, I detoured to the north and followed the gentle sweep of the Kennet river toward London.

It was a cool but perfect spring day, and the trees that lined the road were bursting into leaf with an almost tropical fervor. In honor of the season, I drove with the windows down, and the air smelled sweetly of rain and soil and growing things.

My arthritic but trustworthy Peugeot crested a small hill with a protesting wheeze. Gathering speed, I negotiated a broad curve where the road dipped down into a shallow valley before crossing over the Kennet via a narrow stone bridge. As I bumped across the bridge, I felt a faint tingling sensation sweep across the back of my neck, and my fingers tightened on the wheel in anticipation.

The most surprising thing was that I wasn't at all surprised, this time, to see the house. Somehow, I almost expected it to be there.

I slowed the car to a crawl, then pulled off the road and stopped altogether, just opposite the long gravel drive. A large ginger cat stalked haughtily across the road without so much as glancing at me, and disappeared into the waving grass. Three times in one lifetime, I told myself, even without the cat, was definitely beyond the bounds of ordinary coincidence.

Surely, I reasoned, whoever owned the house wouldn't mind terribly if I just took a casual peek around . . . ? As I hesitated, biting my lip, a flock of starlings rose in a beating cloud from the field beside me, gathered and wheeled once above the grey stone house, and then was gone.

For me, that was the deciding factor. Along with my mother's looks, I had also inherited the superstitious nature of her Cornish ancestors, and the starlings were a good luck omen of my own invention. From my earliest childhood, whenever I had seen a flock of them it meant that something wonderful was about to happen. My brother Tom repeatedly tried to point out the flaw in this belief, by reminding me that starlings in the English countryside were not exactly uncommon, and that their link to my happiness could only be random at best. I remained unconvinced. I only knew that the starlings had never steered me wrong, and watching them turn now and rise above the house I suddenly made a decision.

Five minutes later I was sitting in the offices of Ridley and Stewart, Estate Agents. I confess I don't remember much about that afternoon. I do recall a confusing blur of conversation, with Mr. Ridley rambling on about legal matters, conveyances and searches and the like, but I wasn't really listening.

"You're quite certain," Mr. Ridley had asked me, "that you don't want to view the property, first?"

"I've seen it," I'd assured him. To be honest, there seemed no need for such formalities. It was, after all, my house. My house. I was still hugging the knowledge tightly, like a child hugs a present, when I knocked on the door of the rectory of St. Stephen's, Elderwel, Hampshire, that evening.

"Congratulate me, Vicar." I grinned at my brother's startled face. "We're practically neighbors. I just bought a house in Wiltshire."

And don't miss these electrifying romances from Bantam Books, on sale in September:

THE PERFECT MISTRESS
by Betina Krahn

CHASE THE SUN
by Rosanne Bittner

FROM A DISTANCE
by Peggy Webb

DON'T MISS THESE FABULOUS
BANTAM WOMEN'S FICTION TITLES

On Sale in August

LORD OF THE DRAGON

by Suzanne Robinson
"One author whose star is rising fast!"
—*Romantic Times*

Heartstoppingly romantic, dangerously erotic, and filled with the vivid period details that bring an era to life, Suzanne Robinson's captivating novels have made her one of the reigning stars of historical romance. In her latest enticing novel, a willful beauty and a vengeful knight cross swords. ____ 56345-9 $5.50/$6.99 in Canada

MARIANA

by Susanna Kearsley
Winner of the Catherine Cookson Fiction Prize

A mesmerizing time-travel romance in the tradition of Diana Gabaldon, this richly atmospheric, deliciously suspenseful tale of time travel marks the debut of a spectacular new talent. With miraculous ease, Susanna Kearsley draws us into the heart of a heroine we won't soon forget, in a novel that may be one of the most hauntingly beautiful love stories of the year.

____ 57376-4 $5.50/$6.99 in Canada

DON'T MISS THESE FABULOUS
BANTAM WOMEN'S FICTION TITLES

On Sale in September

THE PERFECT MISTRESS
by BETINA KRAHN

National bestselling author of *The Last Bachelor*

"Krahn has a delightful, smart touch." —*Publishers Weekly*

The Perfect Mistress is the perfect new romance from the author of *The Last Bachelor.* The daughter of an exquisite London courtesan, beautiful and candid Gabrielle Le Coeur is determined to make a different life for herself—staid, respectable . . . *married.* Pierce St. James is a libertine viscount who intends to stay single and free of the hypocrisy of Victorian society. For Gabrielle, there is only one way out of the life her mother has planned for her—she must become the virginal "mistress" of London's most notorious rake.   ____ 56523-0 $5.99/$7.99

CHASE THE SUN
by ROSANNE BITTNER

Award-winning author of *The Forever Tree*

"Power, passion, tragedy, and triumph are Rosanne Bittner's hallmarks. Again and again, she brings readers to tears." —*Romantic Times*

Rosanne Bittner has captured our hearts with her novels of the American frontier. Passionate and poignant, this captivating epic resonates with the heartbreak and courage of two cultures whose destinies would bring them into conflict again and again as a new nation was formed.   ____ 56995-3 $5.99/$7.99

FROM A DISTANCE
by PEGGY WEBB

"Ms. Webb plays on all our heartstrings." —*Romantic Times*

In the tradition of Karen Robards, Peggy Webb offers her most compelling love story yet. From small-town Mississippi to exotic Hawaii to the verdant jungles of Africa, here is the enthralling tale of one remarkable woman's struggle with forbidden passion and heartbreaking betrayal.   ____ 56974-0 $5.50/$6.99

Ask for these books at your local bookstore or use this page to order.

Please send me the books I have checked above. I am enclosing $____ (add $2.50 to cover postage and handling). Send check or money order, no cash or C.O.D.'s, please.

Name _____

Address _____

City/State/Zip _____

Send order to: Bantam Books, Dept. FN159, 2451 S. Wolf Rd., Des Plaines, IL 60018
Allow four to six weeks for delivery.

Prices and availability subject to change without notice.   FN 159 9/95